Jim Crace

THE GIFT OF STONES

VINTAGE

Published by Vintage 1997

2 4 6 8 10 9 7 5 3 1

Copyright © 1988 Jim Crace

The right of Jim Crace to be identified as the
author of this work has been asserted by him in accordance
with the Copyright, Designs and Patents Act, 1988

First published in Great Britain by
Secker & Warburg 1988

Vintage
Random House, 20 Vauxhall Bridge Road,
London SW1V 2SA

Random House Australia (Pty) Limited
20 Alfred Street, Milsons Point, Sydney
New South Wales 2061, Australia

Random House New Zealand Limited
18 Poland Road, Glenfield,
Auckland 10, New Zealand

Random House South Africa (Pty) Limited
Endulini, 5A Jubilee Road, Parktown 2193,
South Africa

Random House UK Limited Reg. No. 954009

A CIP catalogue record for this book
is available from the British Library

ISBN 0 7493 9577 X

Papers used by Random House UK Ltd are natural, recy-
clable products made from wood grown in sustainable
forests. The manufacturing processes conform to the
environmental regulations of the country of origin

Printed and bound in Great Britain by
Cox & Wyman, Reading, Berkshire

£3-50

THE GIFT OF STONES

Jim Crace is the author of *Continent, Arcadia, Signals of Distress* and *Quarantine*. He has won the Whitbread First Novel Prize, the E. M. Forster Award, the Guardian Fiction Prize and the GAP International Prize for Literature. His novels have been translated into fourteen languages. Jim Crace lives in Birmingham with his wife and two children.

BY JIM CRACE

I asked my boys to search and sort the flints in the spoil heap by the mine. They had high hopes of finding implements, a broken arrow-head at least. All they found, in fact, was the skeletal lower arm of a child. Marks on the hinge joint of the ulna suggested that it had been removed by surgery of some kind. We sent the bones across to Carter for some tests – and then we entertained ourselves that night, in the darkness of our tents, inventing reasons why the arm was there, and what the fate had been of that child's other bones.

Sir Harry Penn Butler, *Digs and Diversions –*
Memoirs of an Excavationist (1927)

1

MY FATHER'S RIGHT ARM ENDED not in a hand but, at the elbow, in a bony swelling. Think of a pollard tree in silhouette. That was my father's stump. Its skin was drawn tight across the bone and tucked frowning into the hole left by the missing lower joint. The indented scar was like those made in the ice by boys with stones – a small uneven puncture, wet with brackish pus. The arm was rarely dry or free from pain. As he grew older it would seem (he said) that his wasted and unsummoned semen had found less rewarding outlets from his body than he would have wished. He picked it rolled and spongy from the corners of his eyes after sleep. It gathered on his tongue and stretched into stringy tresses when he laughed or spoke. It formed white blisters on his lips, on his thighs, between his toes. It dried and hardened in his nostrils. And it formed pools of sap in the vents of his severed elbow.

He would invent tales to explain the injury. The arm was taken by a drunk and hungry traveller who mistook it for a chicken. Or it came away at his birth when the women, made impatient by their night-long vigil, tugged too hard upon it. Or it was torn free by an animal – no one knows its name. One bite.

I – his daughter and his only child – took his most frequent, detailed repetition as the truth. It was less fantastic than his other tales and his expression, in its narration, lacked the usual mannerisms of the story-teller, the floating eyebrow, the single, restless hand, the dramatic contours of the voice. He was small and young. The tides were forming crosses on the sandspit. The wind was twisting untidy braids in the manes of horses. The bracken was brown with blood. I can retell it word for word.

At dawn some men had come on horseback to trade. What they wanted, they said, were arrow-heads, some spear-stones, some tools. They had heard that those made in the village were the very best. And, in exchange, what could they offer? The stoneworkers looked in vain for the sides of deer, the skins, the livestock, the cheeses, the baskets of emmer grain which were the usual tokens of trade. These men had none. All they carried were their bows and staves. Dismount at the edge of the village, they were asked. Leave your horses in the care of boys. But they refused. They rode instead between the homes. They clapped their hands like children, calling out obscenities and threats. This is the trade that they would offer: for arrow-heads and spear-stones and tools they promised the villagers a year of freedom from attack. Acquiesce, they said, or we will take this village from you.

"Of course, we simply turned our backs," said my father. "They could shout and shake their sticks and rear their horses at our doors until night came for all we cared. They could help themselves to our village and its stone. Then what? Could they work it? Could they fashion what they wanted from the shattered, clumsy pieces of rough flint which were carried from our pits?" He rehearsed for us the scripture of our village – that we could not be touched because we possessed the gift of stones. If all that the outside world needed was to pound and crush and hammer like savages then any rock would do. But once they wanted more, to pierce and slice, to cut and scrape, to remove the flesh from the inner side of pelts for making clothes, to have harpoons and arrows light and sharp enough to fly and kill, to cut back wheat with just one sickle-stroke, then they, those farmers, horsemen, fishers, wrights, could not be free of us and we were safe. "Our skills had made us arrogant," my father said. "But let the truth be told. Anyone can ride a horse and shake a stick. There are men enough for that and some to spare."

It was his misfortune to be walking from the beach when the men on their horses rode empty-handed from the village. He had with him in a sling a dozen scallops which he had hunted with his toes in the sandspit between the tides. He liked the springy, bracken path that led up from the crusty boulders of the shore, with the wind and spray at his back, spitting and whispering, "Go home to your house and fire. Go home." So he was in no mood – and of no age – to treat the horsemen with suspicion or to roll into the undergrowth when they called him over to them.

Here, perhaps, a picture of my father as a boy should take its place between the bracken and the riders and the sea. It was his seventh year and though there were children of his own age and younger whose weight and muscles had matured, he was still a bulrush of a boy, a stem, his elbows – both elbows, still – thinner than his arms, his chest as flat and formless as a slate. His cousins said his face was disobedient and dreamy, a combination which they found more than doubly irritating. Perhaps it was this challenge and this indifference in his face which caused the riders to treat him roughly. They paced their horses round him and one put out his hand to take the scallops. My father was small and fast and unafraid of horses. He rolled beneath a mare and disappeared into the bracken. And then he showed himself again, standing and jeering on a rock where the horses could not reach.

The picture is incomplete. What he did not see, what only now I can construct in my imagination and place a little distance from the horses, was one other man, dismounted, bow raised and drawn, arrow loosed. It struck the boy, my father, in the arm below the elbow in the arc of flesh which hangs like cobwebs from the bone. It broke the skin but did not enter. Its flight had been uneven. Its head was far too crude and heavy for the sapling reed which was its shaft. But then, what could it matter? The skin was pierced and the goat's purge or the urchin milk or the silverdew which provided venom for the point had mingled with his blood and he was all but dead.

It is better to bleed than not to bleed when there is poison in your blood. My father put his own knife to his wrist and cut a line, half-heartedly, across the three mauve filaments beneath the skin.

Give us the details, we, his audience, would say. Tell us once again how your blood flowed like a cliff spring down your arm, into the sling, onto the scallops, how the landscape turned from bracken-brown to red, how the bracts on the under-leaves stuck to the thickening blood as you toppled from the rock. Tell us, too, about the rich foliage that would have grown, coddled, germinated by the blood. What mushrooms, toadstools; what grubs, what flies, might have flourished there if you had simply fallen and not staggered to your feet again?

That one dismounted man, the bowman barely twice my father's age, had come blundering through the bracken to retrieve his arrow and – who can tell – to put an end to that small boy. My father had sense enough to know the meaning of the stave that the bowman was swinging in his hands and strength enough to run.

Here my father's voice would drop as he, the skilful story-teller, detailed the list of those sensations which gave power to his flight. The bracken, snapping underfoot like kindling to a flame, the bowman's broken bracken gaining on the boy's. The hubbub of the riders and their mounts. The wind, "Go home. Go home. To your houses. And your stone." My father's lungs, his blood, his elbow. The resolutions for the future that he made. His dry and swollen tongue of fear.

There was a moment when the bowman reached the rock from which my father had fallen when his choice was either to continue the chase or to stop and search for that poisoned sapling reed and stone. The world was full of boys that he could chase and kill, but an arrow was of value. It could make its heavy, winding flight again, ten, twenty times. You can't eat boys, but an arrow can stop a deer, a seal, a hen. You can barter arrows for some honey, say, or skin. There is no trade in dead and skinny boys. That, then, is where the bowman stopped the chase and knelt in the undergrowth. Where was his arrow? He found the scallops. He wiped the blood which had stuck to them on the mosses and the grasses and put them in his purse. And then he set to work on the vegetation with his stave, beating at it in a circle and looking for the polished rose and yellow of the arrow's shaft. He did not find it. He could not find it. My father held it in his one good hand and was running with it to our village.

I cannot guess what spiteful, foolish instinct had made father pause to stoop and take it from the ground. But there was some sense of triumph there, as he made a bloodied return to his people, that he had doubly vexed the stranger with the bow. "That man had lost the chase and he had lost an arrow, too," my father said. "Some compensation for the blood and scallops which I had lost, and his poison in my arm."

His neighbours passed the arrow-head from hand to hand and shook their heads and laughed. They knew this stone. Greywacke. Picked out of the gravels, the shales and mudstones, on some river-bank and worked on by an amateur. Here were the flattened planes where the stone had been pounded. Here was a fracture at the arrow's stem. Here were the impact dents where the hammer stone had struck the parent stone sending random chips and dust into the eyes, no doubt, of some muscular, hasty manufacturer who had not grasped that simple truth that stones are broken not by the power of the hammer. Stones are like scallop shells, like nuts. A clumsy, heavy blow will shatter them. One gentle, well aimed strike with a wooden pin and they will open for you like a gate.

Yet what clumsy tool was this? A small boy could do better. No wonder that the horsemen wanted trade if all the stones and arrows that they had were worked so poorly. They would be back, for sure, and with better trade than threats. If they came again and my father lived, the bowman could be asked to provide some recompense.

I will not tire you with my father's recollections of the fever and the pain that followed. He had saved his own life, it was said, because he cut himself below the arrow wound.

Any poison had dispersed. But he had lost much strength and the wounds were slow to bind. His wrist and elbow began to swell and then his fingers became both stiff and shaking. By noon the colour of the skin had changed and, if his arm was pressed, clear water which smelt like damp earth bubbled through fissures to the surface. Soon the pain transferred itself to his upper arm and there were no feelings below the elbow. It was then that he was told that he must lose an arm or die.

2

IT HAD BEEN MY FATHER'S task, some months before the arrow struck his arm, to help with the opening of a new shaft on the hill beyond the village. All the boys and girls were ordered there. It was their job to stand in line with baskets and tip the disturbed topsoil – and the useless stones, the surface flints made unworkable by frost – into disused workings. What they sought was the undisturbed floorstone of flint at depths unknown to worms. This was the act that underpinned the village. If the stone was good then there were profits to be made. The hefters and the craftsmen, the women in the workshops pacing the five-pointed star between the spit, the anvil, the bellows, the cradle, and the pot, could expect good prices for their finished flints from the traders in the market-place. This is how it worked: there were two breeds existing side by side, the stoneys and the mongers, the villagers who dug and worked the flint, the traders who hawked and peddled it with the world beyond.

"You'll never guess," my father said, "which breed was fat and wealthy, which gave the orders, which named the price, which (for the opening of that new shaft) did not stand and shiver in the line with baskets full of earth."

The stoneys' children had been told to start at dawn. It was the light that woke them, and then the noise as all the able-bodied people cleared their throats and noses for the day or stretched their limbs or greeted their families and their neighbours. It was another working day but an exciting one for the children there. The usual routines could be discarded. The village and the workshops would be empty until the new shaft had been dug and the quality of the new stone tested.

The hill was reached by taking paths across the coastal, cliff-top bracken until a bluff of chalk with seams of flint was met. Then the paths converged as there was only one route forward, a steep track with two rock sentries. The youngsters reached it first and for reasons of their age took the gradient at a sprint. Behind, the older men and women, still half-awake on this latest day of labour, were less eager to begin. They made their way through the bracken, some singly, some in pairs, so that to a hawk – be grateful to my father for the image – their progress would seem like a waterfall of people, a dozen slow streams meeting in an impatient, fresh cascade.

My father's ornateness as a story-teller cannot obscure the one plain truth that needs no hawk for decoration – that the village was obsessed with work, with industry, with craft. It made the people purposeful, wealthy, strong. It made them weary too, and a little jealous of the outside world beyond the hill, beyond the warren of mine-shafts, its drifts of un-worked flint.

"There were outsiders close by on that morning," said my father. "As we came onto the hill, breathless from the climb, all could see a distant, breakfast fire, plaiting a rope of smoke for the sky. There was the sneeze of tethered horses. There was the smell of meat."

Here, perhaps, we should raise an eyebrow. Beware of father's tongue. He has led us in his story to the hill and what we might expect is some detail of the labour there, the firing

9

of the grass and gorse and heather, the loosening of the turf, the breaking of the chalk, the shifting of the stones as a hundred people went to work, the tedium. Instead, my father said, he slipped away. No one missed him. He walked towards the smoke. The men there called him over. They let him feed the horses with long grass. They gave him bread and rabbit. There was more laughter amongst these dozen than amongst the hundred on the hill. They blew birdsong with blades of grass. They were in no hurry to begin the business of their day.

Later they put him on a horse and rode away from the coast. He visited their encampment of houses made from skin and wood and played with boys of his own age whose hair was long and tempers short. Some time later he returned to the hill along the landmarks that he had noted in the morning, the fallen tree, the rookery, the clearing with the spongy path, the bluff. The villagers were hard at work. Men were disappearing underground to shoulder-height and loosening the chalk with antler picks for the children and the women to load in baskets and dispose. No one had remarked on his departure or greeted his return. For all they knew or cared he had been relieving himself behind a bush. That was his day of labour. And though our eyebrows may be raised when we consider the facts that father conjured for us, the challenge that he made was this: Who there, amongst the hundred on the hill, did not take a journey on that day? The eye is focused on the stone that must be lifted to the shoulder and then pushed onto the broken turf at the rim of the pit. And then the next stone. And the next stone too. All day. That is how the job is done. The body is engaged. But the mind is like the hawk that father summoned for the image of the paths and the waterfall. It can fly. If one of the men had clapped his hands at one instant in the deepening of the pit and asked, "Where are you?", not one would answer, "Hard at work upon the hill." They were elsewhere. Kings and heroes. Young again. Out at sea. In love. Winning arguments that they had lost the night before. Eating well. Rich. Walking in the forest to the plume of smoke that beckoned there. Hunting scallops with their toes.

3

THE FLINT FROM THAT NEW pit was smoky brown with mottles in grey and yellow. My father's generation was practised in the sorting of the stone. Its colour did not count. It was from weight and form that the villagers could tell with half a glance the way the stone would split, which piece would hold firm for an axe-head, which would fracture into scrapers, which were the most suitable for sling-shot, what to keep for best, what to jettison at once, where the sharpest blade was seated in the planes and fissures of the stone.

Now, with an amputation on their hands and with a dying boy, stunned and mewling from the pain and poison in his arm, they searched amongst the unworked flint with care. What was needed was a knife with an edge so fine that it could sever father's elbow, cut the sinew and the flesh in such a way that any wound would mend. Anyone who has plucked and split a chicken for the spit will know how hard it is to separate the meat and bone, to snap a wing or leg cleanly at the joint and separate the limb. It is best done cooked and with the teeth. (And here, of course, if there were children in his audience, my father would not resist the obvious embellishment to his tale, that this was his fate too. They cooked his raw and living flesh over the fire and removed his poisoned arm with forty bites. There were the teeth marks still. He would present his puckered stump – not too slowly, not too close. And, indeed, you thought you saw the logic to his lies – those indentations, those pussy fissures and frowning scars could be the work of mouths.)

But once again it is the plainer story that we favour, the one which places father on his bed, semi-conscious, weak, his elbow pierced and swollen, his wrist and hand caked in blood from the morning's black and self-inflicted wound. Someone stood and rubbed water on his forehead, on his lips. Nothing could be done until a knife was made.

A stone was chosen from the spoils of the new pit. It was hoof-shaped with a tendon-like ridge running from its ankle. With luck there was a good blade within, but tools do not simply drop from flints like pips from pods. The patience and the artistry of a craftsman is what it takes. And some luck, too. And, as luck would have it, there was a craftsman in the village at that time renowned for the sharpness of his blades. Renowned also for the bluntness of his tongue, his dolefulness, rigidity. I will not say his family name for my father never used it. Behind his back he called him Leaf, like all the other boys. The reason is no mystery. This man would always keep a leaf upon his bench. He could replicate its shape in flint, its texture almost, its autumn colours, its patina. He aimed to match its thickness, too, its thinness. But its weight? Would he ever come that close?

Leaf was the man given the task of fashioning the amputation knife. Here it is certain that my father's version of events was cake of his own making. How could he have known how Leaf went to work and the problems that the craftsman met – my father was dreaming, dying in another house. He could scarcely brush away a fly. So here I must

abduct my father's story for a while and spend some time –
as father never would – talking of our village skill with flints.
We have before us, on a bench placed in the good light of a
workshop yard, a hoof of stone.

This is a moment of great patience. Leaf would not wish
to work the flint too soon despite the boy and his condition.
He had first to picture in his mind's eye the type of blade, its
length, its weight, most suited for the amputation.

Leaf's huts were on the windy brow of the village, above
the beach and sea. But we should not picture him walking
to the shore, absently popping the wrack, or even looking
out to sea to gain his working focus and his inspiration.
He did not like the beach with its unruly rocks, its colonies
of weed, its changing shape. If he could he would have
squared it off. Where was the utility of the sea? What was
its symmetry?

Our village looked inland. We were not fishermen. Fish
was bad to eat – though gulls' eggs, crabs and shells were
welcome in the spring. And we were not sailors either. The
sea brought no one luck and so we stayed away. Lives were
passed in this one place, working stone and seeking respite
from the wind. For the villagers then, a still day was a day
when their hair simply lifted from their foreheads. It didn't
tug their scalps. It didn't slap their faces. And so we should
picture Leaf in that short time before he struck the flint,
crouching for protection behind the wall of his workshop
yard, holding a wet finger to the cracks to check for draughts,
pushing fussy wads of moss between the stones, vainly
wiping strands of hair across his head (for he was almost
bald), and imagining the perfect blade that he would make.
His youngest daughter had lit the fire with driftwood and

with bracken. Its flames hardly danced. Leaf's walls had all but stunned the wind.

He took the flint and turned it in his hands. Would it do for such a task? Leaf wanted even-textured, predictable stone. Flawless stone. He wanted stone that would not shatter but would fracture at the point that he dictated. All looked well enough. He moved his daughter from the fire and placed the unworked flint into the ashes and the flames. She brought the bellows and pumped heat into the fire. The grey and yellow mottles on the flint darkened to match the brown. Leaf squatted at his daughter's side and watched. He dare not let the flint turn black. It could split or splinter. But he wanted a hot stone, one that could be worked easily and precisely and at speed, one that would open from the delicate, controlled impact of the softest hammer. Cold stone was resistant to the gentle arts of knapping. Hot stone was best. His daughter brought two long slates from his basket of tools. Once her father had sat on his stool with a flat stone anvil on his knees, she retrieved the heated flint with her slate tongs. She put it on the anvil and, spacing her legs for a firmer stance, held the stone in place. "Now all that stood between me and death," said father, relishing his circumstance "was a hoof of roasted stone and a hairless, trembling Leaf."

4

LEAF'S FIRST BLOWS WERE SIMPLE ones, and hardly trembling. He had to form a rough but tidy core from the quarried flint so that it would sit firmly on his anvil. One blow with a crude stone hammer removed the flint's grey rind. Another squared its base. A third removed a nugget of intrusive chalk. It was a simple matter requiring not skill or strength, but confidence. The core stone that remained would have served elsewhere, in some less sophisticated place, as an implement in itself. You could club a man to death with such a stone, or crack nuts. Where was the craft in that? But how to make a knife? Where to begin?

Untutored hands would muster all their energy and smack the hammer on the flint. With luck, there might be tiny scrapers accidently made that would serve as barbs for arrows or for cleaning skins. But only one stone, thus struck, in twenty thousand would provide, by chance, a long, strong splinter for a blade. Craftsmen – cautious, focused, their tongues curled and dry – would take their time. They would seek to understand the stone, to know its valleys and its hills. That tendon-like ridge on the hoof of stone – was it the length and thickness, would it serve as a blank for the amputation knife? Could it be detached easily from the core?

Leaf placed his sharpened antler tine on the flint, exactly where the tendon was attached, and struck it with a wooden mallet. These were the perfect tools but only in hands like Leaf's that were firm and certain. If the direction of his impact were a feather's breadth too shallow the fracture would surface too soon. The knife blade would be shorter than a thumb. It would be chisel-shaped. Or, if the impact were a feather's breadth too deep, the fracture would plunge so that its blade end curved in a lumpy hook, a talon, a beak, a keel. Who'd want a poisoned arm removed with that?

For Leaf himself there was no tension. He knew what to do. He'd done it many times. One blow and the blade blank broke loose, spiralled for an instant on the anvil and fell into the apron on Leaf's lap. There, on its underside at the point of impact, was the distinctive raised tump of stone, like a tiny bulb or a winkle shell. Beyond, in the foothills of the tump, the flint feathered and radiated like a slow tide on a flat beach. It was a good, long blade, still warm from the fire.

Once again Leaf and his daughter returned the stone to the flames. Leaf exercised his hands and – half-exultant, half-impatient – blew out his cheeks to match the working of the bellows. He chose the best tools from his workshop for turning the blank into a finished blade. He sat, with a different, lighter anvil on his knees, to receive the hot stone. Again he worked with antler tines but with no hammer. A little sideways pressure removed the tump, the shell, the bulb. More pressure produced a mounting nest of fine and shallow flakes on the anvil as the blade was patterned and reduced.

Enough, you say. A boy awaits. The afternoon has almost gone. There is no need to detail the patience and the expertise with which Leaf etched a pattern of shallow facets along the cutting edge, or how the flint's parallel flaking scars were ground ice-flat with grains of sandstone, or how the stoneworker reconciled his quest for beauty, symmetry, utility with the urgency of his task. If there had been time he would have cut a block of ash and made a handle for such a knife. He would have fixed the blade into the ash with birch resin. It takes two days to harden. He would have worried at the flint until it had lost all resemblance to stone. As it was he simply rubbed the blade in grease, to boast its natural colours and to catch the light, and – picking up a few sharp scraps from the flake nest on his anvil – delivered his newest tool to the crowd who waited at his gate. He was not patient with their flattery. The blade was good, for sure. It'd do the job. But he was aggravated by the thought of what the new knife might have been were there time to finish. It would have been a tool too fine to use. It would have been an ornament.

5

THOSE OF US WHO HAVE kicked an anthill will understand the chaos in the village. The dreaming ants, so used to patterns and to chores, had been sent wild and spirited by the unheralded disorder of the day and by this thin excuse to shout and smile and swagger. In the causeway between the huts and workshops, where normally at that hour in the afternoon there were only hens and children, the crowd was advancing with the amputation knife. Faces, which usually were white with dust and concentration from the shaping of the flint, were flushed and restive and keen to play a part. Voices were high and unrestrained. There were wars of jostling and of tripping in that crowd. It was as if the sober stoneys were all drunk and far too blithe to care exactly what it was that brought them there but only glad to be involved.

There was a mood of unexpected celebration, too – not because the wounded boy – my father – was considered careless, indolent, untrustworthy, the sort who only had himself to blame for any ill-luck in his life, but because their rigid working day had been disrupted by the horsemen, by the making of the knife, by the prospect of a bloody afternoon.

Who would carry out the operation? There were no volunteers. There was no man or woman among the villagers who could boast experience in such matters. And there was no time to fetch some expert from the outside world, some butcher-herbalist or adept knapper of the flesh. My father's version of events expertly shapes a symmetry between his dying body on the bed – the stillness of the bulrush boy, with the blackening blood, the paling skin, the cold and sweaty forehead – and the bluster of the villagers faced with a task beyond their skills. A balding volunteer was quickly nominated, one who was not present in that room and so could hardly make his case for staying absent. Leaf should carry out the amputation, someone said. He'd made the knife. He would know its properties. Besides, he was the finest craftsman of them all. He had a steady hand. Compared to making leafs of stone it would be a quick and simple task for him to shorten this boy's arm.

Once again the crowd set off – this time, uphill, into the wind, towards the ocean brow. Come on, Leaf, they called. There's work for you. No one was fool enough to specify. But Leaf would not leave his workshop – where he sat, another anvil on his knees, excavating oysters – until he knew the story. And then he wouldn't move at all. He had no ambitions as a carver, was all that he would say. He had his lunch to eat. He'd done his share and made the knife. No more. Find some other sap to chop the boy in two.

At last, of course, partly persuaded by the accusations that his reticence was merely cunning, that his knife was blunt and splintered and could not amputate a toadstool let alone an arm, Leaf was persuaded to leave his shellfish and his workshop and set off, downwind, towards – he thought – the dying, poisoned, bloodless boy. Meanwhile my father, for some reason unexplained and inappropriate for his condition, had begun to feel quite well again. His arm was painful, but the sleep had restored his spirits and reduced his fever. He sat up upon his bed and wondered what there was to eat about the house. He wondered, too, what all the noise was in the causeway beyond the wall. Slowly the possibility occurred that he would not need to lose his arm at all.

His revival was not widely welcomed. Leaf and his companions were not relieved to see their patient standing at the gate, his expression once again the usual stew of idleness and insolence, his arm hanging heavily at his side. His liveliness presented them with problems. "He should be down and out," said Leaf. "I can't cut a boy who's half-awake. He has to be unconscious." Some beer would have done the trick for a boy of father's size. Or – better – a cup of wood spirit or headspin made from grain. But this was the village of stone where work and trade were king and queen. No one got drunk, no one had drink. The fabric of the village was made strong by the warp and weft of rules. Intoxicating drink was not allowed. It produced bad flint.

They returned my father to his bed and debated their difficulty. Here they had a boy whose arm was damaged beyond repair. If they did not swiftly put Leaf's knife to use, first his shoulder, then his chest would succumb to the poison in the elbow. It might take hours, it could take weeks – but finally the boy would die. There is a limit to what can be cut away. You can't remove a shoulder and a chest. But with a cussedness that matched his usual manner the boy was conscious. How could they put an end to that? There were those amongst them – Leaf included – who harboured thoughts that perhaps the village would be no weaker if the boy did die. He'd never make the best of workers. He had no love of stone. He spent too long idly on the beach, or in the woods. Such thoughts, of course, were left unvoiced. The warp and weft again demanded that the boy be saved. And now.

It is not difficult to stun a sheep. A blow to the head with a wooden mallet is known to quiet the beast for the butcher's knife. So it was with father. They thought they'd knock him out. Here the tale presents a boy of seven, already bloody from a wounded arm, stood up by men twice, three, four times his age and battered round the head. One misjudged fist blow to his nose caused more blood to flow. One mallet blow to his brow (to which, by now, we must add my father's terror and his sobbing) brought up an instant, broken bruise in the shallow flesh above the skull. A last desperate finger chop to the nape of his neck caused the perpetrator more damage than the boy. He was not stunned. It was a scene too rough and comic to seem cruel. Those men who could strike a flint and dislocate its core with the force and delicacy of owls hunting mice and shrews could not bludgeon one small boy to sleep. It was a foreign craft.

Here I am tempted to infiltrate my own concocted version of those moments in the past. I knew my father and his neighbours. Timid is the word. They could not strike a boy in such a heartless way. I imagine them frozen and hesitant at the very thought of it. The fist drawn back would not unleash itself. The raised mallet would be held back by the force of custom. Theirs was an ordered, working village. Scrapping was for cockerels.

It was at this moment, then, (my father cowering but untouched, Leaf's new knife untested, the dusk upon them) that the horsemen of that morning returned to the village with goods to trade. They left their horses, as requested, in the care of children and proceeded on foot between the huts and workshops to the market green.

It would be an error to imagine that just because a small boy had been injured and that a crowd had gathered for the amputation, that the working life of the villagers had ended for the day. There are those who cannot settle and for whom any occurrence is excuse enough to form a crowd. But there are others, too, who never let their focus shift. The world could split in half and still they'd have their noses pointing down at the work bench or the stall. And so it was that the horsemen found a reduced but busy market-place on their return and merchants there whose outrage at the wounding of a village boy was swiftly tamed by the usual courtesies of trade. Except, of course, that the crudely struck arrow-head that had caused such hilarity in the morning was prominently displayed amongst the local, finer tools so that the horsemen might understand exactly what debts there were to pay. Yet far from embarrassment at the rediscovery of their arrow-head these men were jocular. They pointed at the head and chuckled. So there it is, they seemed to say. They'd spent a lot of time in vain knocking back the bracken. They expressed no interest in the boy who'd last been seen in flight. In fact these horsemen did not seem reliable, predictable in any way. There was much laughter amongst them, and warmth and swagger, too. Their hair was long. Their clothes were decorated. The expression in their eyes was bold and childlike. They seemed at ease – yet wayward, loud and unrestrained.

Everybody there was drawn towards this knot of men. The villagers were hypnotized, and for a while the trade in borers, burins, sharpeners, harpoons, stone wrist-guards, sickles, fire-flints, sling-stones, scrapers, hand-axes, arrow-heads and tangs and barbs came to a pause. Women stopped their basketry. Small boys who fashioned string by rubbing buckleaf fibre on their thighs finished early for the day. The man who sold coloured dyes which came, he said, from snails and molluscs, bark, insects, the waste of certain birds (but which, my father claimed, were lightning dust) ceased for once to sing his wares. Visitors from far away who'd come to trade with fat-hen weed or honey, with herbs or decorated bone and slate, cups and birch-wood boxes, with shells, wood, shellfish, nuts, sloes, pears, peas, apples, round cakes, flour, clothes, with frogs and brownies from the stream, forgot the purpose of their journeys. Piles of clay pots, antlers, charcoal, willow fish-traps, nets of hens were left without attendance. Everyone – except the opportunists – came to watch the fun.

We knew that you'd be back, they told the horsemen. We knew that once you'd seen the flints that we make in this village you'd want to talk with us, not fight. Now, what's on offer?

The horsemen sat amongst the mats. Candles were brought and dishes of curd. A skin-bag was collected from the tethered horses and emptied at the merchants' feet. There were five hollowed lengths of femur bone, cut from the carcasses of deer. Each had been stained yellow and then carved with flower heads in crowded, perfect detail and linked with filaments and lines, so that the surface of the bone was frost and lichen interlaced. It was the sort of pattern, finely traced by insects, that could be found beneath the loosened bark of trees. For the knappers in the market-place the bone-work was the finest they had seen. They crowded round to rub their thumbs along the yellow, decorated shafts. Yet no one was fool enough to speak out loud the price they'd pay for such ornaments. Instead they shook their heads and said, No use to us. What could we do with these?

One of the riders – a man as old and bald as Leaf – gathered up the bones from the rubbing thumbs around him and placed all but one before him on the mat. He took a finger of flat wood and, holding the bone high in the candlelight so that all could see, he scraped a plug of hardened fat from the bone's hollow. Now he was careful that no one else should grasp the bone. He held it upright at his nose and sniffed. Perfume, he said. Those villagers who stood behind his back could lean forward and see a blinking disc of green fluid and smell the unmistakable fume of orris plus the honeyed redolences of new, dramatic odours. It made their hearts beat fast. It made them blush and pass uneasy smiles. The bone of perfume was passed across to those traders whose flints the horsemen had inspected. They assumed the expressions of experts as they each lifted the perfume to their nostrils and, a little shakily, passed on the bone. Their mouths were watering. Their eyes were cloudy. One, at least, shifted uneasily where he sat to disguise a sudden, unheralded erection. A little touch of this behind my wife's ear, a smudge between the breasts, he thought, a dab between the thighs. Another, made suddenly breathless and urgent for transaction by the fragrance in the bone, could manage his palpitations and impatience only by sneezing like a horse. Here was something that defied reason. A sneeze and an erection were both appropriate ripostes.

Where is this perfume from, they asked. The horsemen shrugged. They weren't completely sure. We didn't ask, they said. We simply saw the opportunity and helped ourselves.

There was a caravan, beyond the forests, a dozen days from here. They'd traded horses for some skins. And then, at night, armed only with a knife they had crept up on the sleeping caravan and cut the horses loose. They weren't ashamed of that. It was reclamation only, hardly theft. They'd found the skin-bag with its decorated bones strapped to the blankets of a horse. One had splintered and there was perfume on the horse's flanks. They spoke what every man was feeling – that even a horse, with perfume like that upon its flanks, could make a man keen-set.

The properties of the goods for barter were now declared. Here was perfume of the strongest kind. Here were vials of decorated bone unparalleled for beauty. Here were arrow-heads, spear-stones, tools which, when compared to those made elsewhere (and here a clumsy arrow-head was indicated and tuts exchanged) were sharp, light, fast, strong and shapely. The traders recommended an exchange – five decorated perfume bones for twenty arrow-heads, three spear-stones and a tongue-shaped axe with a good thick butt. After some time and some concessions, the bargain was agreed. They clapped hands to bring it to an end. The horsemen put their flints in the skin-bag and handed over the hollowed deer bones. Once more they clapped hands – and that would have been the end of that exchange had not one man, barely twice my father's age, leant forward to retrieve the ugly stone which he had last seen that morning as it dipped and laboured from his bow.

Now that the barter was at an end, the restraints and etiquettes of trade could be set aside. One of the knappers, his head still spinning from the scent, surprised himself and his companions with a sudden, half-considered act. He kicked the arrow-head away – and its owner toppled foolishly upon the mat. Here the horsemen were at a comic disadvantage. They were dismounted. One of their number was face down. They had transgressed, they were reminded, not only in the unseemly efforts to regain the arrow-head, but also in the damage done that morning. (Now everyone was startled at the plainness of the words.) There was a boy, not far away, they said, in pain and dying. It was the horsemen's fault. They ought to make their bowman provide some recompense. You think we're fooling now, they said. Come on, we'll show you what a careless bow can do. The traders and the knappers there, with the horsemen at their centre, amused and hardly fearful, now set off for the place where my father lay. There they joined their unsettled, work-shy neighbours who had formed the first crowd of that day and demanded entrance to the room. The boy was conscious, standing, his injured arm bloodied, swollen and inert. The bowman smiled.

6

HERE THEN WAS THE STRANGEST recompense. It was a simple matter for the riders from beyond the hill, much used to drinking, perfume, quarrels, horsetheft, wars, to first give father too much drink from their leather travel-mates of spirit and then to strike him neatly on the chin. The softest blow, not a feather's breadth too shallow, not a feather's breadth too deep, flicked my father's head back on his spine. He spiralled, fell. "It was my first encounter," father said, "with our good friend Hard Drink."

They took his arm off, too. They were used to amputations. Their family dead were dismembered and buried in a pot. It was less trouble than digging graves or building chambers under earth. It was not only dead limbs, either, that they were used to cutting. One horseman lifted up a hand with two fingers and a thumb half gone as evidence that they could take a knife to living people, too. They were often fighting, casually with strangers, and there were many wounds. The body held no mystery for them. Leaf was happy to pass on the task and watch the experts with his knife. First they tied a leather strap above my father's elbow. Clear earthen pus burst from the swollen upper arm. Briefly some colour returned to his limb and then beyond the elbow joint it turned the inner blue of mussel shells. A second leather strap was tied higher on the arm and a slat of wood was rested on my father's chest as a working surface. They put his arm upon it and strapped it to the wood with ropes. They threw spirit on his arm. His skin was cut and opened with those few sharp scraps that Leaf had gathered from the flake nest on his anvil. An uneven thin red line was cut. My father flinched and moved his arm in sleep.

Those who expected a scarlet eruption, a cascade, were disappointed. The straps held father's blood at bay. The horseman with the knife was now impatient. With the strong and even strokes of a deer-hunter stripping and salting meat, he cut into the flesh with Leaf's new flint. The bunched stem of arteries and nerves was the most resistant, but the three boyish muscles which enfolded it gave way before Leaf's perfect edge like wet peat. The audience had never seen such colours. With so sharp a knife it was a speedy task to separate the knuckles of the higher bone from the two long bones below the elbow. With a belch of clear and bitter fluid the unhinged lower arm came free. Its bluish tones had paled. It was no colour. It matched my father's face. Bury it, the cutter said. My father's arm was gone. Leaf put out his hand to retrieve the knife. I'll keep it, said the cutter. That leaves us even on the day.

There is no need, I think, to embroider this much more. It was dark by now. The horsemen – boastful and jostling with the villagers – had to ride away. They had their flints. They'd paid their recompense. All in all they'd had a lively day. My father was unconscious on the bed, drunk and bruised and dreaming. The bleeding was quickly stemmed with wood smoke. Maggots of the screw-worm fly would be brought and placed upon his wound to accelerate the healing. The skin would stretch and pucker, frown upon the world.

And it would drip its poison and its undiminished pus forever like tree sap, like semen, like a punctured boil.

My father's story, then, of how he lost his arm presents a village briefly gone awry. We must retain the image of a normal day, the workshops busy with the rhythm of bone and wood and stone, the causeways quiet and empty except for children delivering new flints, the market-place a murmur of transaction as wheat and skin and pots changed sides with axes, spears and knives. The anthill was at work, measured, skilful, dull, secure. To this we add the day's disruptions – a heavy arrow, the wind and manes of horses, the trepidations of a dying boy, the perfume and the decorated bones, the taste of spirit on my father's dreaming lips. How were people on that night? Were there better tales to tell across the hearth as hot, flat stones were made ready for the meat? Were children silent, tense? Was there more passion in the hearts and beds of those who'd watched the horsemen mount and ride off to the night? My father had it so. He drew for us a portrait of our home and village sent skittish by these unin- vited guests, their gifts. Children were conceived that night. Subversive thoughts were aired at the expense of traders, flint, the drudgery of work, the slavery of skill. Maybe, even, blows were struck and quarrels made and mended with a hug. The man who'd kicked away the bowman's arrow-head made the most of that, telling and retelling what he'd done, perfecting every detail. His midnight version was the best: Who said that bowman toppled to the ground, he asked. I plucked him up myself and tossed him there.

And then, of course, the embers died. The village slept. It woke as usual with the dawn and slowly, painstakingly, more flints were formed; the hammers, scrapers, bellows, chisels were gathered up and put to work. Here was the normal day – except, of course, for one small boy who slept on and on for fear of waking to his pain – his severed arm caked and stiffened by dry blood, his nightmares blustery and full of stone.

7

"LISTEN HERE, *(MY FATHER SAID)*. I'll tell you what occurred. I'll keep it simple, too. I won't tell lies. So don't expect some bristling story of revenge, the sort retold in whispers after dark about the boy who killed the lambing wolf or the wife who drowned her husband's secret friend or the feuding sons. There is revenge to come, for sure. Malice and my elbow stump are twins. But at that moment when – seven years of age – I watched the bowman's smile, there was no revenge in my mind. Children aren't like that. They are more subtle. Is that the word? Or is 'simple' closer to it? Let's hear it then, let's tell the truth: the sum of my ambition at that time was not to kill the bowman for the damage he had done, but to be the bowman, to be on horseback in the wind like him, to let the heavy arrow fly at anything I wished, to struggle loose from stone.

Let me describe his face as best I can. You'd think it was a leather purse with teeth. You never saw his eyes. He had a horseman's squint. He was only young, but he was weathered as a piece of bark. Sometimes my memory conjures up a small moustache, sometimes a scar above his lip. I can't be sure. It was years ago and I have told this story many times and changed it just as often. But one thing never changed. The bowman's face, his smile, his eyes, expressed in full what neighbours in our village had most distrusted in my own face.

Look, you see it now, a little blunted, true . . . but dreams
. . . but turbulence . . . but downright cussedness. He could
have been my brother.

So is this my story then? Watch out, you say, he's
chipping and he's knapping at the truth. He's shaping it to
make a tale. Two brothers. Separated at their birth. And
reunited. In a feud. I'll spare you that. I'll save that story for
the children late one night, and we'll get on with something
less exciting.

So I was seven, almost dead, but tough and cussed, too,
and on the mend. My chin was bruised. The skin was broken
on my head. I'd lost a lot of blood. My lower arm, my hand
– the one I used for eating, fighting, wiping arses – was snug
and damp somewhere beneath a rock. Or flung from the cliff
top into the wind. Gull food. Or – this is likely – disposed of
on the hill beyond the village. Down some disused pit. The
hill was full of holes. I'm buried there. A bit of me, at least.

Who cared for me? At first it was the uncle who'd sobbed
out shallow promises to my dying mother when I was small.
'See to the boy,' she'd said. Uncle kept his word. He'd raised
me as his own. That means I shared the slappings that he
gave to his six sons and daughters and his wife. That means
that I was underfed and generally ignored unless there was a
job to do, some lift or fetch and carry. But, when he heard that
I was wounded and that my arm was briefly famous, he showed
himself the model of devotion. He was among the men who
volunteered to knock me out. It was his mallet on my brow.

But then, next day, my arm was off and it was clear that
I would live and thrive. He moved me to his huts on a stretcher
– my cousins shared the weight – and, on the way, took every
chance to sing his praises. Make way, make way, Uncle All

Heart passes through. We rested in the market-place – and there we found the world returned to normal. The disturbances of yesterday were done. There were no horsemen there. The hollowed bones of scent had gone. Don't ask me where. There was a stir of interest in my stump – but that was their curiosity at full stretch. Why should they care? There were no scabs for them to pick. What's done is done and soon forgotten, unless there's debt involved.

My uncle and his family lived frugally. He wasn't good with flints. His best were simple mallets, hammers, axes, implements without a blade. They were hardly highly prized amongst the traders in the market-place. The gift that made Leaf rich made uncle curse. He had no patience. He was a bear. You should have seen him hard at work. You'd think his hands were feet. One pair of working hands, he'd say. Eight mouths to feed. Mine made it nine. His plan had been that his six children and I, his sister's child, should join the workforce speedily. Eight pairs of working hands – he didn't count his wife – could make him rich and fat. Now he wasn't slow to see, as I lay recovering in his huts, that my recent loss, my half a pair, would not advance his plan. What kind of knapper would I make with my best arm ending in a stump? His girls could learn to work the stone, he said. They could do it just as well as boys. But me? What could I do? Get in the way, that's all. I couldn't fetch and carry any more. One arm was not enough for heavy stones. I couldn't work the bellows; two handles need two hands. I couldn't dig for flint. I couldn't strike a tine and split a stone unless I held the hammer in my teeth.

So I grew up like some wild plant, ragged, unattended, not-much-use. While my domesticated cousins learned from uncle how to bludgeon stones, discovered how to cluck and chivy at their work all day, I learned how to irritate, discovered how to peck and knap at tempers. I was the magpie, they were hens. No one came to me and said, You've lost an arm, so what? You've got another on the left. Let's see it work. It can be done. Come on, sit down and trap the stone upon the anvil with your stump. Or, here's the way the one-armed master goes to work; he changes crafts. He becomes the herdsman or the cook, the leatherman. His cheeses are the best. His goats. His perfect-fitting shoes. No one said, there are a thousand things to do that don't require two arms. It takes one arm and two good legs to take a bucket to the stream and bring it back, unspilt. Do that. Or four fingers and a thumb are easily enough to take up keeping bees.

The simple truth is this, no one had the time or inclination to find a role for me. Making flints, that's all they knew. That's what gave them heart. That was the ritual which kept them going, that filled their time, that stocked their larders, that gave them pride. Work made them comfortable. It made them feel, We do exist, We are important even, We count. They were the stoneys, heart and mind. They blindly fashioned flints. And gulls laid top-heavy eggs. And the winds blew off the sea. That's how the world was made and never pause for thought. It wasn't made for boys with stumps.

I promised you there'd be no lies, but you'll excuse excursions and short cuts. What is the profit in listing here the countless days I fled the cursings of my uncle and my cousins to laze about the village staring idly into other people's lives? Days spent doing nothing, when I was eight, nine, ten, could slow this story down. You'd fall asleep, you'd topple to the ground, if I told that. You'd dislocate your jaw with yawns if I recounted here the casual, endless rebuffs upon which my boyish indignation fed. I stalked the village like a homeless pup, unnamed, unnoticed, empty, cold, uncombed, and loved by no one but itself.

So, seven, eight years on. I was beyond the bowman's age. It was the end of summer and there you see me once again upon the shore, running toes along the sand. I was well. I had no colds. My throat was clear, my lips were soft. For once the wind and sea were tame, the wrack was almost dry, the birds were grazing on the beach like sheep. There were no living scallops at my feet, just empty valves, the fluted valleys of their fifteen ribs turned green and black with seacrust. I could invent for you a sea and wind and sky that flung saltweed in my face and emptied water from the pools and cast a light so dark and feeble that even lugworms took the day for night, mistook the wind for tide, and coiled their ropes too soon upon the sand. But I will keep it calm and windless. The sight was no less strange. I skimmed a scallop out to sea and there, as unselfconscious as a cloud, a ship was passing by.

What would you do if you were me? Run back and tell the stoneys? What? That they should arm themselves and gather on the shore? That they should hurry from their work-shops – the stones left baking, the bellows breathless in the hearth – and prepare themselves for trade with sailors? That they should simply stand in awe, like me, and witness from the land the recklessness of travel on the sea? They'd tell me, Scram. We've work to do. They'd call me Little Liar. And, for sure, if one or two were tempted to take the bracken path towards the sea to prove me false, they couldn't reach the cliffs in time. For all the stillness on the beach, the muscles in the clothing of the sail made clear enough to me that there were breezes just offshore. That ship would soon be out of sight. Unless, of course, I followed it. Why shouldn't I? I had no stones. I simply filled my chest with air and took off down the coast.''

8

"THE SEA VIEWED FROM THE clifftop is a world that's upside down. Its gulls have backs. You're looking down on wind. The shallows, from above, are flat and patterned, green with arcs of white where the water runs to phlegm. My ship threw up an arc of its own phlegm as it dipped and bounced before the wind. I bounced and dipped myself. We were a pair. At times the ship sank out of sight, lost in the trenches of the water. More often it was I who dropped from sight. The clifftop path was cut by wolves and goats. It made no sense. At times it ran, ankle-deep, as straight as sunlight across thickets of winkle-berries. My one hand dipped and picked. I breakfasted on fruit. But then, when ferns and brambles were dominant, and low flat trees with antlers of greying lichen on their sheltered barks, the goats and packs of wolves split up. Their paths ran out. I did the best I could, but made mistakes. I finished up on rocky promontories where going on meant sprouting wings. I found good downward paths to silent coves which offered no escape except by going back. I fell from rocks. I cut my shins. At least I wasn't lost. No one that I knew from my village had been this far before, but getting back would not be hard. I'd trampled down a path. Any fool could turn about and follow clifftops home.

Already, in my mind, I knew the story I could tell that

night – that I had tracked the ship until it turned across the wind and came ashore. Then what? I'd see. My only certainty was that if I blundered on I'd greet the sailors on some beach. It was a certainty that did not falter when the wind began to quicken, the sky turned toadstool-grey, and the arcs of phlegm upon the sea-shore curled to spit against the beach. I hurried on. I hurried on, despite the undulations of the path, despite the growing distance of the sail. People on their own do foolish things. They don't know when to stop. They don't know how. Now you understand why people live in villages, sniffing at their neighbours' cooking and their conversations. They fear themselves and what would happen if the leash were cut and they were all alone.

Of course, you've guessed. A boy, half-man, can't race a ship. I dropped into a valley where a stream spread out amongst the tumbled boulders of a beach and then climbed through mallows, brambles, bracken, moss until the sea was wide again. The ship had gone. I waited for the trenches in the water to surface, rise and flatten, and for the distant sail to signal in the wind. But all I saw were black waterhuggers flying singly for their ledges and the brows of seals as they came inshore for shelter and for rest. There was just a chance, I thought, that sailors were like seals, that when the winds blew hard and the sky grew dark they turned their own brows to the land and sought the safety of a beach. Perhaps there was a spot ahead where ships could put ashore. I should have turned myself and sought the safety – and indifference – of my uncle's huts. I walked a few steps back towards our village. It was no good. The wind – now armed with flints of rain – was in my face. I turned my back against the wind. I carried on. I ran.

The landscape changed. It was not cliffs and coves. Low heathland swept gently to the shore where thrift and black-tufted lichens lived side by side on rocks with barnacles and limpets. There were clumps of seablite, flourishing on spray. There was arrow grass and milkwort. All the herbs and medicines and dye-plants that we saw bunched and dried and up for barter in the market-place were in abundance here. It made sense to gather some on the journey home and offer it as evidence that I could earn my keep. At last I could admit that I would not reach the ship. The coastline was in view for quite a distance. There were no sails. I collected seablite for its purple fleshy leaves. Good for stews and dyeing wool. It is not easy to harvest plants whose roots are tough enough to withstand wind and sea when you have one arm and everything is wet. You tug too hard and slip and damage what you pick. I soon gave up. I'd go home empty-handed but with purpled fingers.

It was when I sought some shelter from the rain that I noticed all the rocks. I found a place beneath an overhang of heath which was still dry and protected from the wind. I sat there, looking out to sea, uncertain what to do. And then I saw the colour of the stone. Juice-red like elderberry stain. I'd not seen that before. Arrow-heads and knives in red would cause a stir. I'd bring my uncle here and my six cousins. We'd carry rocks back home.

I chose a piece about hand-sized and wedged it between my feet, its upper, rounder face well clear. I did not expect to make a tool. I simply thought that I would test the blades and edges at its core. I hit it with a stone of equal weight and size and colour. One blow. Both stones – the one in my left hand, the one between my feet – broke open and apart. They crumbled like a fist of clay. It felt as if I'd brought two drinking pots together. All I had was shards, none bigger than my thumb-nail. I tried it once again, with different stones. More shards. More random piles of stone.

I cannot say how foolish and how alarmed I felt, sat there, seduced away from a little food and warmth by one lost ship, my one hand red from seablite, the seashore red with stone. I had encountered there a rock unknown to all my neighbours. A stone so soft – I soon would learn – that the sea could break it up. A stone so soft it couldn't crack a skull. Was this some illness, some disease? Imagine if the illness spread, if it made its way along the coast to infiltrate the flint pits on the heath. A picture came into my mind which left me smiling and breathless with its implications. Leaf's youngest daughter was carrying a heated stone, a juice red stone, across the workshop. She placed it on her father's anvil on his knees and, spacing her legs for a firmer stance, held the stone in place. Leaf positioned his sharpened antler tine upon the stone, his hands as steady as his eye, and struck it with a wooden mallet, certain of his craft and grateful for the chance to work on something new."

9

"IN FACT, IT MIGHT HAVE been a dream. I fell asleep, my head upon my hand. The walking and the wind had tired me out. When I awoke I couldn't see the sea, I couldn't tell the colour of the rocks. There was a mist and it was dusk and all that mattered was the distance from our village and the fear of being stranded in the night. You'd all be just as fearful, that's for sure. The beach is fine by daylight, but at night it is too open and too cold. There might be wolves. There might be worse. And yet to walk back along the cliffs could not be done. I'd fall. I'd shred myself on thorns. I'd drown in rain and blackness and in leaves. I stood and looked inland across the heath. I filled my lungs with damp and heavy air. 'Who's there?' I said. And then I raised my voice and called, 'Who's there?'

I was answered by a dog. Its bark was wolflike for an instant. My stomach and my bowels made soup. My legs gave way. I'd never known such fear, not even when young leather-purse, the bowman, had come blundering through the bracken to retrieve his arrow, his stave circling in the air, my right arm lost. That was in the day, and I was close to home. Now I stood as still as stone, breathing through an open mouth and planning what I would do when the pack had sniffed me out. I'd run into the sea. Would that have done the trick? Can wolves swim? I wouldn't know.

There were no wolves. There was another bark, high-pitched and servile. It was a single dog. And there behind its call, just lit and barely visible, the grey on grey, was a streaming plume of smoke.

Now you see me running on the saltland heath, sending rabbits to their burrows, putting up the roosting birds. I didn't care. There was a smudge of safety in the air. If there were fires and dogs then people were close by. I'd pass the night with them. They wouldn't harm a one-armed man, a youth, a boy. I'd eat, sleep, go home in light. I'd take an elderberry stone."

10

"ALL WE HAD TO EAT that night was slott. The woman ground the fish eggs into creamy paste and added green flour. She rolled the mixture into dumplings and heated them in sea water on the dampened fire which she had lit too dangerously close to the reedwork of her hut.

'Watch the pot,' she said. 'Don't let it crack. And call me when they're done.'

'When are they done?'

'They'll rise and float,' she said. She took a cup of water and stooped to leave the hut. In the dull light that lingered in the distance I watched her step into the grasses with her dog and walk a little way from the hut. She wore a belted smock. She took it by the hem, lifted it up to her breasts and squatted on the ground. Beneath the smock, she was thin and naked. Her buttocks and her thighs were creased and empty like punctured water bags. The hair between her legs was long and black. The dog stood before her, its tail erect, sniffing at the ground. She took its muzzle in her hands and pushed the dog away towards the hut. Her eyes were good. She saw me watching her as she added earth to earth, and cleaned herself with the water and some leaves. 'Watch that pot,' she called, and pulled a screen of grass to block my view.

The dumplings were still boulders at the bottom of the sea. I turned my head away from the woman in the grass and looked about her home. Her child was sleeping on its mat. I could hear the snort and whistle of its blocked nostrils, the insect in its chest. The woman's woven house had once been strong, but water, winter, sun, wind and frost had soaked and dried and split and snapped the reeds. Its coating of caked mud had cracked and fallen. Its roof required new timber. Its floor, fresh mats. The bracken fronds that she had used in bunches on the ground to keep out draughts and rats wheezed and fidgeted with bugs and roaches. Now I saw the sense in lighting fires so close. What smoke remained blew low into the hut, into my eyes, into the baby's chest, into the bracken and kept the flies away.

'Are they done?' she said. She was standing at the fireside, her smock in place, the dog sniffing at her hands.

'Not yet.'

'You're not much use.' She shook the clay pot with a stick and the slott came up like bubbles in a pool. She tipped the pot and let the water run away until there were only dumplings and a little juice. She reached for some dry wood which was stacked inside the hut and for a while we had a golden flame without much smoke by which to eat our meal. She looked much older in that light. Sockets large and rimmed from sleeplessness, lips cracked and ulcerated, hair coarse and bunched in stooks behind her ears, white sores in clusters on her nose. I'd seen her skin before. It had the points and peaks of urchin shells. I've said her eyes were good. Quite clear and grey and unabashed. She handed me hot dumplings.

'They're good,' she said, but she did not eat with appetite. She ate as if it were a duty. She had good cause. The taste was high and tedious.

'We had much better food,' she said, 'when my husband

was around. We had our pick. Crab, we had. And laver soup. And samphire, too. That tastes so good. He picked it at low tide in summer from the marshes over there.' She hardly moved her head. 'You have to let the roots hang for a while before you cook. And then you strip it with your teeth. You eat the flesh and throw the stem into the fire. It whines and bubbles there like spit. We had all sorts of fish. He caught them in those baskets.' Again she hardly moved her head to indicate the fish traps, holed and ageing, hanging from the roof. Her voice woke up the baby. It was a girl. She crawled onto her mother's lap but would not take the salty pellets of slott which her mother offered on a finger. She lived in the hope of milk and nuzzled at the smock until her mother pushed it from her shoulders to her waist and let her suck. Her breasts were scarcely more than nipples. 'There is no milk,' she said, and shrugged. She must have known that I was watching her, a youth who'd never seen a woman naked and so close.

I see you smile and brighten up as if you think I'll tell some tale of how I dropped my head, perhaps, and took the woman's other nipple in my mouth. Or, throwing down my dumpling, put my one good hand upon her knee. Hard luck. You have ignored the state that she was in, the ulcers and the dirt, her thinness and her poverty. What I said about her eyes – quite clear, and grey, and unabashed – has made you think of sex. Me, too. She was a beauty in decay. And I was cold and wet and far from home and frightened of the night.

She was obsessed with food. She went on talking with the baby tugging drily at her breast: 'When my husband was still here we'd eat so well. Lobsters, coalfish, ebb meat. We never eat the same thing twice. Baked eel. Baked guillemot.

Seakale. Goose eggs. Have you had those? Have you had mussels roasted in hot stones?' She told how her husband and her two boys would scour the sea-shore for its fruits, how they would search the cliffs for nests, and harvest reeds, and club the seals to death. Once they found a whale, a rorqual, on the beach. There was meat and hide enough to feed and clothe a hundred men. And fat for light, and bones for fuel, and ribs for making huts. They took the surplus – the whale, the eggs, the kale, the tasty saltland rabbits – to the markets at the villages around – and they came back with meat and milk and cheese and beans and beer.

'On market days we had a feast,' she said. And then, one day when they had gone to trade at the village where the stoneys lived, they did not return. The dog came back. But not her husband or the boys. She waited. She was waiting still. Who knows what happened to them. She went herself to the village. 'I've never seen such things,' she said. 'Such wealth. Such homes. But the people there. . . .' She mimed some spit. 'They had no time for me. I came back here. I had this child, poor thing. I do the best I can. I have the dog. I do a little trade. But I never caught a fish. No one taught me how. I never clubbed a seal. I couldn't climb a cliff for eggs. So I make do. I found a dead fish on the shore today, its eggs were swollen in its pouch. This slott has been a treat. And then? Perhaps my family will come back and we'll eat well again before we die.'

I asked her, had she seen a ship? She shook her head. She hadn't seen a ship. All she'd seen that day was me, emerging through the heathgrass with a look of terror on my face. I'd looked so frightened of her dog and so burdened with the rain that she had no choice but to offer help.

'And that?' she asked. She nodded at my severed arm. 'What happened to the rest?'

What happened to your husband and your sons, I thought. The same, no doubt. If I could lose an arm for a dozen scallops, then they could lose their lives for whale meat, rabbits, kale.

'My arm?' I said. 'I lost it at my birth. You know what mothers are. Mine couldn't wait and pulled me out, and snap. It came away. You don't like that? Then, let it be an animal that tore it free. Half-dog, half-gull. No one knows its name. One bite.'

Why tell the truth when lies are more amusing, when lies can make the listener shake her head and laugh – and cough – and roll her eyes? People are like stones. You strike them right, they open up like shells.''

11

"WE ALL SLEPT WELL ENOUGH. The dog was reassuring and the baby far too weak and underfed to do much else but suck and doze. I spent the morning on the marshes by the shore. There was no hurry to get home – by 'home' (so far) I mean the village, not the smoky hut. And there was samphire in abundance, a little past its best, but a favourite of the woman and a gift from me.

When I returned there was a single horseman waiting in the grass beyond the hut. The woman with her baby and the dog was talking to him. He gave her something which hung still and then began to flap. A chicken, upside down and twined up at its feet. She walked towards me and my gift of samphire. 'Please help,' she said. She handed me the chicken and the child and made me hold the dog back by its neck. 'It won't take long,' she said.

I stood and watched and she rejoined the horseman. He dismounted and they walked into the longer grass. I watched her as she took her belted smock by the hem and pulled it high and off above her head. She stood there, thin and naked once again, the horseman's hands upon her waist. With her good eyes she turned and watched me watching her. 'Go inside,' she called. 'Can't you kill a chicken?' I did not move. They lay down on the earth. This time it was the horseman who pulled a screen of grass to block my view."

12

"YOU SEE? I'VE PULLED A screen of grass across the story, too. I'll not creep up and tell you what I saw. I'll spare myself – and her. Now you know, you can be sure, that this is truth – no chronicler with any sense would disappoint his listeners so. The narrative would buzz and hover like a gnat above the horseman and his whore. We'd watch his buttocks, double-dumplings, and her knees. We'd follow their duet. Instead, you'll hear from me a solo of lament. I felt – in charge of dog and child and hen – as if she'd let me down. Betrayed.

I'll beat it out as simply as I can. That night just past had been the calmest in my life. I'd found an audience at last. We'd dined on slott beside the romance of a fire. Her dozing baby and her breasts, the dismal meanness of her hut, the dog, the wind, and (more than that) the age of her which made her sweetheart-mother-sister interlaced, a braid, had filled my head with countless expectations. She hadn't cared about my arm. Or knapping flints. Or stone. She'd said, Do this. Do that. Make sure that pot is safe. Here, take the child. And hold the dog. Can't you kill a chicken? Could you walk down – take this bag – and pull some samphire roots? Before, I'd only ever idly stared through doors to watch the workers shaping stone, to smell their smells, to watch their lives while waiting for the Scram, Get out, We've work to do. And so, you see, the smallest dumpling, cooked with patience, given with a smile, could make a servant out of me, could make me lose my heart.

I had imagined . . . naturally, who wouldn't? . . . that, given time, the pumping buttocks in the grass would be my own. And not for trade in hens. Now once again the simple sum of my ambition was not to kill a horseman but to be a horseman – though shooting arrows of a different kind. Fat chance.

I turned my back. I put the baby on her mat. I tied the dog. I released the chicken from its twine. I set it free. The child began to cry; the dog to whimper, then to bark. The hen took off. And so did I. I walked down to the shore and found the overhang of heath where I had sat and smashed the rocks one day before. I waited there. But she did not come. I searched the skyline for a ship. No ship. I set my face against the wind and almost ran. It was not yet dusk when I reached the bracken path above our village. Had I been missed? The plumes of smoke were lifting from the workshop fires. There was the pant of bellows. The air was prickly with the click of stone on stone. My people were at work. I felt as if my life was cursed with failure and misfortune."

13

"'WHERE HAVE YOU BEEN?' My uncle shouted. He had become a trader in the spring of that same year. While his sons and daughters laboured in the workshops – and while his mutilated nephew roamed at will – he had found himself a spot in the circle of transaction at the centre of the village. His flints, arranged upon a mat, were crude and cheap and plentiful. His trading pitch was just as rough. His voice was rasping, his chest was full of chalk – flint-knapper's lung, they called it. Between the spits and coughs, he holla'd and he crowed at any passing farmer with eggs to trade. Or any girl with cloth. Or any craftsman loaded down with pots or baskets. He'd found his talent. He'd been placed on earth to strut and shout. He was the market's cock.

So, the 'Where have you been?' which greeted me on my return was not a question seeking answers, a demonstration of concern. It was a piece of drama for the mongers and the pedlars there. Gather round, it said. We'll have some fun – and while we're at it we'll do a little business, too.

'You see? He has no answers?' uncle said, pulling me to his side so that all of those who looked at me would see his axe-heads too.

'Where has he been? He disappeared like that. No word. No by-your-leave. He spent the night . . . who knows? Some girl, I think!' They laughed. 'Some girl who should be warned.

Perhaps, at night, she didn't notice that his hugs comprised of just one arm. He had to add a leg, maybe. He stroked her with his toes. I promise you these flints, these best stone tools, are not the work of toes . . .' And he embarked upon his well rehearsed display.

He tried it once again that night, for the benefit of all my cousins. 'Where were you, then?' he said. I had a question unspoken on my lips, too. Did anyone remember a stranger and two boys? A dog? They came with eggs and kale and tasty saltland rabbits. Once – one, two years ago – they had some whale to trade. Did anyone recall three bodies on the outskirts of the village? Were there rumours of that kind? Did anyone recall?

'I met a woman . . .' I began.

'Ah!' My cousins sniggered as they ate. 'I'll bet she was a beauty . . . with four hooves and horns!'

'I met a woman . . .' I repeated.

'Let's have her name,' said uncle, cheapened by the easy laughs he'd earned that afternoon. 'We ought to let her know, poor girl, that those cuddles that you gave her in the night were done with just one hand. You had to lift a leg and stroke her with your toes.' His repetition was worthwhile. It earned him some applause. He rose and left us to it. But my cousins were entrapped.

'Who was this woman? Where . . . ? Come on. Speak up.'

That was an invitation far too good to miss. I'd tell them all about the old reed hut behind the sea, about the woman and her family and her child, the damp, her poverty, her food. Perhaps – at night, before the dancing flames it didn't seem unlikely – they'd share my sense of sorrow at what went on in the world beyond the hill, the world that had no stone.

But, first, I had to tell them all about the cliff, the beach, the ship upon the sea.

'What would you have done?' I asked, 'if I had come to you and said, Put down your tools, I've seen a ship. You'd tell me, Scram. You'd call me Little Liar!' They laughed at that. They recognized the truth. 'And, anyway, that ship would soon be out of sight. Unless, of course, I followed it. Why shouldn't I? I had no work to do. I simply filled my chest with air and took off down the coast.'

My cousins had stopped eating. Their eyes were turned on me. Those phrases – 'filled my chest' and 'took off down the coast' – had made them hopeful in a way they could not understand. Those phrases were like perfume. They had dramatic odours. They promised more. I knew at once the truth could not be told to them. It was too dull and disappointing. No love, poor food, a woman – thin and naked, with breasts like barnacles – who sold herself for chickens. What could I say to make it sound attractive? They wanted something crafted and well turned. I wanted their applause. The truth would never do. It was too fragile and too glum. It offered no escape.

'The sea seen from the clifftop is a world that's upside down,' I began. I stood and spread my long arm and my short to demonstrate the view I had. I pointed down.

'The gulls have backs. You're looking down on wind. The shallows, from above, are flat and patterned, green with arcs of white where the water runs to phlegm. My ship threw up an arc of its own phlegm as it dipped and bounced before the wind. I bounced and dipped myself. We were a pair.'

This is my moment of betrayal, both of the woman and

the truth. Hear how it comes to life. See my cousins, sitting there, their chins aglow with grease, their eyes on fire, their expectations high, their dreams and nightmares on display.

'I caught the ship,' I said. 'It came ashore.'

I told them all about the coastline, how the cliffs died out and sank so that the heathland and the beach were clasped like fingers of two hands. I told them how the white sail of the ship was forced to labour against the tide, of how I waited hidden in a cove where the rocks were elderberry red and elderberry soft. They looked delighted when I said I'd meant to bring some red stone back for them to see, but had forgot. I'd bring some for them in a day or two. They laughed out loud. They loved – and feared – the nerve and challenge of the story-teller."

14

WE BEGGED MY FATHER TO repeat for us the story that he told that night to his audience of cousins. What happened when the ship reached shore? Were there men on board or what? What was the cargo that they brought? He claimed he was not sure, that stories were like dreams, like dragonflies. They came and went. They only gave one show. His cousins might remember. But he could not. Besides, he'd told a hundred versions since – and no two were quite the same.

We have heard my father talking – and we know the way he worked. We know that when he spoke he shaped the truth, he trimmed, he stretched, he decorated. He was to truth what every stoney was to untouched flint, a fashioner, a god. We know that when he said, "I'll keep it simple too, I won't tell lies," that this was just another arrow from his shaft by which we were transfixed. And so, again, we should beware when father claimed forgetfulness and said "Who knows what story I dished up for them that night? Who cares?" He knew, for sure. It was a turning-point for him – though, here again, his version was much tidier than truth. His version said that that one tale, told late at night to cousins, had kicked the anthill once again. He'd startled everyone; he'd surprised himself. It was as if the village fool had, unannounced, stood up and juggled perfectly – or the stammerer had sung a faultless song. It was a revelation and a shock that in the village, hidden, uncultivated all these years, there had been this amputee, who now could hold a household silent with the magic of his words.

The truth for what it's worth is this . . . and now I'm guessing, so can you see the value of my truth? . . . my father's talent for inflating and for telling lies was always there, from birth. But no one guessed its power – until, that is, my father transformed his defect into craft. As the bully becomes soldier, and the meany becomes merchant, so the liar becomes bard. Where is the shock in that? But father had it thus: that one good story from his mouth transformed him in that village, overnight, from the wild plant, not-much-use, into their raconteur.

His cousins spread the news. Their Little Liar had a tale to tell, they said. He'd chased a boat and caught it too! And then – guess what! – the sailors all were women. And their cargo? Perfume, stored in jars the shape of birds with necks for spouts. And then they'd come ashore, and then and then. . . . And so the story was passed on. Of course, next day, the stoneys and the mongers in the village called out to him, What's this we hear? And father was obliged to stop and tell his story once again.

He could not, he said, have invented a more workable device for telling tales than the ship upon the sea. Each time it came ashore it could offload a new and untried plot; a different set of characters with untold loves and enmities could disembark. The ship had formed a rough and tidy core from which my father could detach at will his patterned blades of fable, romance, lies.

Come on, they said. What's this about the women? My

father soon became adept at shaping what he said to match the shining eyes of listeners. The groups of men who hung around the market-green, far from their wives and children, were keen to hear a tale which flirted and which teased, which offered sex and trade. You know the appetites of men. My father could oblige. For them his ship offloaded girls with one thing on their minds. They were like sirens – and the perfume that they came to trade was like a drug that stupefied all men. He'd hidden in the rocks and watched as merchants and their sons from the villages around had come down to the beach. They laid their merchandise among the wracks and urchins, between the salt heath and the sea. They made high claims for the cloth, the charcoal, and the pots which they offered for exchange. The sailors had no need to speak. They dabbed some perfume on their wrists, their necks, their breasts and offered one sniff to the noses of the men. Those men – the youngest and the fittest – who did not faint and drop like overhoneyed bees, were offered more than sniffs. The sailors led them to the longer grass beyond the beach. . . .

And then? my father's audience inquired. What then? Of course, he would not say. The power of a tale is in the gaps and pauses. I hear his voice. I know his tricks. And there is a phrase that comes to mind which father often used. "We'll never know," he'd say. "We can but guess. A young man and a woman in the grass. What could they do but hunt out insects in the soil, or teach each other songs, or sleep? I couldn't say. I didn't creep up close enough to see. And anyway they pulled a screen of grass to block my view."

His audience applauded. He had delighted them. Their minds – so used to earthbound things – had flown, danced,

like larks, like gnats, with father's tale. They knew full well –
if there were ships and women sailors armed with odours of
that kind – what would have happened in the grass. They
knew, imagined, what they'd have done . . . if only life was
like a story, simpler, freer, less ordained.

My father paused for larks and gnats to settle, and then
he held a finger up and halved his voice to double their
attention. "Be warned," he said, "if ever that ship puts to
shore near us." His story had not ended with the transactions
in the grass. There was more to tell. The old men of his story
were unconscious on the beach like washed up seals – the
young and fit were stunned and sated in the grass. What
then? The snare. The sailor-women – chuckling at their power
over men – gathered up the charcoal, cloth and pots that were
on offer there and stowed them in their boat. They took to
sea. What had their cargo cost them? What had the merchants
and their sons to show for their endeavours? Who had been
gulled by whom? My father did not need to say. He had his
hearers spellbound with the questions.

Here was a story custom-made for men. But father took
a chance and told it to the women, too. They loved it even
more. They laughed and held their sides at father's picture of
the slack, defenceless menfolk on the beach and the scheming
women out at sea. He had them nodding at his final words
that "There is a place, between the navel and the knees, where
the wisest men are fools".

For children, gathered in a ring for father to amuse, his
ship contained less physical distractions. The women came
ashore from a craft whose sail and hogging line were stiff and
white with ice. They saw my father hiding in the rocks. They
beckoned him. He went. He had no choice. They were honey;

he was bee. There is no need to fear, they said. We've lost our way. He asked: Where is your destination? The sun, they said. We're sailing to the sun. He said: You'll fry. But they displayed no fear of heat. It's cold we fear, they said, and snow and frost and ice. Already we are cold. Our finger-tips are dead. Our toes. Our ears. If we can reach the sun then we'll be free of fear. Show us where to sail to reach the sun, and we will heap on you rewards that have no name, that are magic, that are as old as time.

And if I cannot? father asked. What then? Then we will turn you into ice, they said. To demonstrate their panic and their power, one of the women sailors lightly touched a tress of oarweed which hung from rock into a pool. One touch and it was ice. A frozen shore-crab toppled free and skated, slid, ten limbs brittle, on the crisp and glinting surface of the rock-hard pool. An anemone which had been red and sinuous became a snout of ice. Its thousand snakes shivered one last time.

"What could I, should I do?" my father asked his audience, enacting every shiver. "I was too cold with fear at what I'd seen and heard to help them on their journey. Does anybody know? What is the best way to the sun?" The children did not know. Up, up, they said. The sky. But father shook his head, for ships don't fly. The routeway must be sea. The children shook their heads as well.

"Come on," my father said. "Speak up! The sailors are impatient. They have to reach the sun. Their fingers are stretched and ready for the task of touching me and turning me to ice. Come on. Come on. I'm going to catch a chill!"

He beckoned with his arm and made the children gather close. He whispered the solution. "The sun was going down upon the sea," he said. "My time was running out." And then . . . of course! The sun. . . . Was going down. . . . Upon the sea. . . . And soon the two would meet! The answer was so simple. He told the sailors to be patient. Stand upon the beach, he said. Each night the sun must sleep. It rests inside the sea. The fishes are its dreams, the tide its breaths. You'll see it fade. And drop. And settle on the water. Sink. You then set sail until you reach the point where you saw the sun go down. You'll find a gaping hole with steaming water all around. Put down your anchor. Wait. And, when the sun goes down that second night, your journey's at an end. Your boat is anchored at the spot where once there was a steaming hole. The sun comes down upon your deck. I promise that you'll never freeze again.

The women watched the sun go down, they watched it bathe and wallow in the sea and throw a cloth across the sky. They thanked my father for his help. We give to you the gift of turning life to ice, they said. And this we give you, too. They tipped a little perfume from a jar into a scallop shell. He smelled it – but the skin upon his nose touched the arc of liquid. It froze. Dissolve it in your mouth, they said, and make a wish. My father sucked. My father wished. He wished he had a healthy arm, four fingers and a thumb. It will come true, the women said.

The children in the ring looked at my father's elbow stump. They saw no magic there. My father looked at it and them, intently, as if he expected the frowning tucks and scars to burst apart and a new arm to emerge. When nothing happened, my father shrugged. "I got it wrong," he said. "Look here." He held his good hand out. "You see? I already have one healthy arm, four fingers and a thumb. I should have asked for two!" The children laughed, but they'd been fooled. They wanted proof that father's tale was true. "I have the proof," my father said. "I have the gift of ice. Which boy, which girl, will step out here and touch me on the hand? Come on. Be brave. If anyone is turned to ice, we'll melt them on the fire." He made as if to pick a child from amongst the crowd. They backed away. They screamed and giggled. They hid. There wasn't one who'd take the chance of proving father's lies were lies.

We do not need to hear my father's other variations, the bespoke stories that he told to tease and stimulate his aunt, his neighbours, his enemies, the old. He was never lost for words. He had a name for everything – or invented one. He'd out-hoot an owl, they said.

And so it was that father became – not liked exactly, or respected – but useful in the village, and admired by some. He could be seen – the irony is rich – inside the sanctum of Leaf's yard reworking folktales for the family as the master sat at anvils and his daughter pumped the fire. You'd meet him, too, at any great occasion, celebrating with a tale the naming of a child or marking death and burial with some fitting yarn. And there were hardly any feasts or meetings of the village which did not feature father fantasizing at the higher table in the hall. Imagine, too, the usefulness of such a skill on market days. His uncle was not slow to make the most of that.

The paradox is this – we do love lies. The truth is dull and half-asleep. But lies are nimble, spirited, alive. And lying is a craft.

"Let us be cruel and listen to that craftsman, Leaf," my father said if he was ever pressed to justify his elevated

standing with some villagers or the applause which marked
his wilder tales.

"Imagine you have spent all day crouched over stone.
Your eyes are tired, your back is stiff. You need to take a stroll
and the way that you have taken leads you to Leaf's workshop.
You lean upon his perfect wall. How was your day? you ask.
You do not care – you simply want to be amused, to hear
another voice that isn't stone on stone."

But Leaf – and this was father's point – could only answer
in one way. He would knock the splinters of chipped flint
from his chin and lips, re-arrange the camouflage of long,
stretched hairs across his head, and simply tell the truth. It
would be flat, his tale. It would take his audience through the
day, his daughter at the bellows, the master at the stone. If
his listeners did not hold their hands aloft and say, Enough,
he'd detail every shallow flake that fell upon his anvil, he'd
have them witness all the tedium of work, each word of his
would be a hammer blow.

"Imagine, now," my father said. "A liar intervenes. He
picks upon the leaf that always rests upon Leaf's bench. Leaf
is too shy, he says, too modest. Today the master's dream
came true. He found a flint which had the colours of this leaf.
It was an oak in stone. He shaped it with the bays and
headlands of this leaf. You see the stem and veins? You see
the curling stalk? Leaf made them all in stone. He made the
flint so light and thin that it began to rustle like a winter leaf
disturbed by wind."

"Should you believe what this deceiver says?" my father
asked. "You are not fools – but you have had a trying day
and he has made you laugh. Only Leaf is not amused. And
that makes you laugh some more. You play the game. You

challenge both these masters – the story-teller and the stoney
– to produce the flint-leaf for inspection. Leaf himself is silent.
What can he say? He's stuck. These lies have made a fool of
him. But the liar is not trapped. He never is. He does not care.
He says: Leaf's leaf was on the table, cooling, lifting at its
edges from the breath of those who came to see it. It would
make Leaf the richest, greatest knapper in the land. And then
what happened? Yes, you've guessed. A bird came in and
took it for its nest. It was so light, this flint, the bird bit through
it with its beak. The pieces floated to the floor like oak ash
drifting from a fire."

Imagine if the liar then invited everyone to look down
on the floor, to get down upon their hands and knees, to find
the pieces of the leaf-in-flint. Everybody would snigger at
his thinness of deception. A leaf-in-flint, indeed! But could
anybody swear, my father asked, that their eyes would not
momentarily dip, their eyelids flicker, their knees give way,
at the prospect of a shattered oak-leaf on the floor? Salute the
liars – they can make the real world disappear and a fresh
world take its place.

"The secret of the story-teller," father said, "is Never
Smile. A straight mouth and a pair of honest eyes is all it takes
to turn a stone to leaf." You've never seen a face like his when
he was telling tales. It was as candid as the moon.

15

THERE WAS ONE CERTAINTY IN what my father told to me. The woman in the hut, her child, the dog – none of these were false. They were not characters from stories. Their tale was far too bleak. "If what I wanted was a woman, I'd not invent one quite like her," he said. He mentioned her to no one there. He put her out of mind. But he could not shake her loose from his imagination. She haunted every story that he told. And every time he looked outwards from the village – towards the sea, towards the heath – it was her grey eyes that he saw, her body in the grass, a horseman's hands upon her waist.

Nothing stopped him now. It was expected, if he chose, that he would disappear again into the outside world. That's where, it seemed, he got his stories from. The villagers imagined him, a hunter, tracking down his tales. He'd soon be back. Some villagers – those elders who mistrusted too much levity, those victims of my father's tongue like Leaf – were quite relieved to see him go. He was disruptive. He had skills that could not be bartered in the market-place. He had no time for stone. Some children were a little frightened of him, too. They did not like the scars and fissures of his arm. They did not trust his tales which, like sling stones, were sharp on every side.

And so, when spring came round, my father crept into

his uncle's yard one night and helped himself to gifts that might please the woman and her child. A wooden top that had been his youngest cousin's. A goat-skin mat. Some nuts, some grain, a good flint-knife. Some scallop candles. A pot. He wrapped them in the skin and tied them to his back. It was a night that only comes in spring. The air was warmer than the earth and, as he trod the usual route along the bracken path between the village and the sea, his feet sent up a puff of frost which turned to mist on contact with the air. In that no-light of moon and stars, it looked as if his feet were shining like a pair of tumbling glow-worms in the damp.

The sea was out. It was the spring low tide, and shore that normally was undersea was breathing air for once and basking in the moon. This was my father's path. He took advantage of the tide. At night it seemed much simpler than the clifftop route, the path of wolves and goats along which he'd blundered in the summer past. He walked barefoot and cursed the pebbles and the weed which made the going both slippery and hard. The sand was worse – it opened up beneath his feet like drifting snow. One arm was not enough for keeping balance. He fell down and the sandprints that he made with hand and feet and knees winked and bubbled as they filled with sea. He'd left the glow-worms on the bracken path. Now his tracks were listless silver spheres which shrank and flattened as the wet sand at their edges collapsed to fill the holes.

Quite soon he found a tidal ridge of shingle which was dry and firm. Now he could walk quickly despite the limpets and the cockleshells, the broken bones of cuttle, the crab claws and the vacant whelks which formed the ridge. From time to

time he felt a movement underfoot – unnerving in that darkness – as foraging sandhoppers, sea slaters, crabs, who knows
what else?, nipped and quivered at his soles. At first he was
not cold. His exertions and the bag across his back preserved
the warmth of his uncle's house at night. But the sweat across
his forehead and his shoulders was soon turned gelid by the
wind which the sleeping land sucked and summoned from
the bleaker sea. Soon he was as cold and damp as frogs. A
little frightened, too. The sea, that night, curled and lisped and
whispered in a voice which said Dismay, Dismay, Dismay. No
wonder that the wind took flight, took fright, and sought the
refuge of the shore. The land was mute – no birds, no human
cries, no sheep, no sign of welcome or of safety to my father
walking on the beach.

If we'd been him we would have turned around and
gone back home. Too cold for expeditions. Too wet. Too dark.
Too treacherous and full of wolves; too pitiless with wind and
whispers. Too void. We'd seek the bracken path again and
creep in to the village, replace the nuts, the knife, the grain
and candles we had stolen, and lay out with our cousins by the
fire. But my father is not us. We do not share his bludgeoned
vanity, his moodiness, his resolution. We do not share his
ardour. He did not turn or run. He walked along the shore
as if his home was close ahead and not behind. He whistled,
hummed. He sang. His voice was whisked away and shred-
ded by the wind. If we had seen him there upon the beach
that night (he said), if we had watched him striding on the
tidal ridge, we'd trust his word that, more than fear, he felt,
for once, exultant.

Of course, his triumph could not last. The landscape and
the tide conspired to chase him off the beach. He rejoined the

cliff path at that point where a valley joined the coast. Its stream spread out (remember?) amongst rocks and tumbled boulders. When he had passed this way before – at the frontier where chickweed turned to wrack, where skylark became tern, where earth gave way to sand – the river water had been warm and shallow. He'd waded it and hardly got his ankles wet. But now, at the finish of the winter rains, the stream was deep and strong. It was too dark to follow inland on the bank until a crossing place was found. Besides, my father was in no mind for deviations or delays. He stripped and put his clothes into the goat-skin wrap. He held it, high and dry, in his good hand and stepped into the water. He didn't fall. Or drop the wrap. Or lose his footing in the stream and end up – moments later – dumped and bruised like flotsam on the beach. Dimly he could see the dry bank on the other side. He fixed his eye on that, kept his legs well spread, and crossed.

By now his teeth were chattering like a conference of knappers' stones. His skin was barnacled with cold. His hand was stiff. He dressed – but all the dampness of the stream was soaked up by his clothes. The wind passed through him: it played his ribs. He was wattle without daub. He took the woman's gifts out from the skin and placed them on the bank. He wrapped the skin around his shoulders and sat amongst his gifts, hunched up, a boulder, with his head upon his knees and his arm around his shins. Now the boulder trembled. He was a logan-stone, shaking on the spot. The noises that he made were icy, animal, dank; they were the rhythmic, shivering inhalations of people making love, or cowering, or cold. His stump – a loather of the cold – was numb. He knew he had to light a fire.

He stood no chance of finding any kindling or dry moss in that light. He took the flint knife that he'd stolen – the sharp and perfect product of his eldest cousin – and tried to cut some kindling from his head. (In his retelling father made it comic, miming with his severed arm and a head that now was old and dry and bald.) But on that night his hair was long enough and coarse and hardly damp. The wind had kept it dry. At first he tried to trap a hank behind his head with his numb stump and to cut the hair free at the roots. He could not hold it firm enough. The hair sprang loose. (He mimed that, too, to laughter that was cautious, thin.) Then he used one hand and tried to slice the thick hair at his forehead. It simply flattened on his skull. Here was a task that required two hands. A one-armed man could only crop his own hair with a knife if he could find the reckless courage to hack the skull, to mutilate his head.

My father put aside the knife. So much for flint and stone! He held a thin hank of hair – forty, fifty strands – between his pointing finger and his thumb. He pulled to test its strength – and then he snapped the hairs out from his head. He was surprised how easily they came, how little pain there was. He tried again. Another skein came free. Quite soon he had a nest of hair – and a head that looked chewed up by rats.

Consider now how hard it was for him to break his cousin's knife in two, to trap the one half with his toes and strike it with the other. Producing sparks was simple – but they were haywire, shortlived, futile. What he needed was ignition, a spark which had the force and foresight to settle on the nest of hair. To simmer, smoke. To smoulder, flare. To blaze.

Depending on his mood – and on the age and temperament of his audience – my father would invent new ways of making fire. A fire-fly came and settled on the hair. A lizard that had flames for breath. A fire-ball. A fire bird. A glow stone. Even with a pair of friction sticks and the dryest moss we know how hard it is to summon fire. With stone and wind and hair? What chance? The truth is this, that father was just lucky. A spark obliged. A few hairs curled and shivered at the thorn of heat.

Fire is determined. Once it has a pinch of life, it flourishes, it thrives. The hairs sent up the sour fume of burning flesh, part crab, part cheese, part gall. They smoked and melted, flared and shrank, became one piece of brittle, sticky tar. Their blaze was strong enough for father – his hand unsteady from the cold – to light the wick of a scallop candle from his store of gifts. He lit them all. Their flames winked and guttered in the wind. My father placed one scallop in the pot to save it from the weather. Its flame reflected on the clay and, from the pot's mouth, released a single, watery pillar of light in which my father thawed his hand.

There were enough dead twigs, damp reeds, dry pith, seed masts, plant waste, bark, close by for father to build up a fire with the scallops at its base and the wooden spinning top – his youngest cousin's treasured toy – at its summit. At first it was all smoke – but the wind took that away and coaxed flames to startle on the twigs. My father was at a loss, he said, to comprehend the depth of pleasure that a fire can give.

He soon was warm, but not all of him at once. That's the trouble with an exposed fire – it scorches cheeks and noses while necks and backs and buttocks are left freezing in the night. My father had to turn himself, a chicken on the spit, to make quite sure that he was thawed right through. And then he sat before his fire and sucked the emmer grain and ate the nuts. Their shells were fed into the fire. And while he sat there, making shapes and stories out of flames, the sun came up behind his back. If he was at a loss to comprehend the depth of pleasure that a fire can give, then what could he make of dawn? It dulled the cutting edge of wind. It brought my father's shivering inhalations to an end. It silenced father's teeth; the knappers' conference of stones was suspended for the day. His wattle now had daub. The logan-stone was still.

My father threw the broken knife and the scorched remains of pot into the ashes of his fire. He wrapped the now-warmed goat skin round his shoulders and set off again upon his travels. He knew the way and climbed up from the valley through the mallows and the brambles – now thickening with promises of leaves and buds – until he reached the high cliff top of bracken. There was no ship upon the sea, just a rose-hip sun with fleshy canopies of cloud. Already shags and waterhuggers were flying off for the day's first fish. Fronds and frost and cobwebs gleamed with dew. Giant slugs were on the path. Rocks steamed.

Father thought then of his cousins and his uncle's hut at dawn. It was still dark inside. Grey slates of light squeezed past partitions, curtains, screens, to rest in tapered, oblong slabs on walls. If there was movement it was rats or an ember settling on the fire. If there was noise it was the rasping in his uncle's chalky lungs. If there was exultation, it was in dreams. It ended when they woke.

My father made too much of this, his celebration on the cliff, his sense of liberty from toil at being up so weatherswept and early with the sun. But what is liberty anyway? Not much more than self-deceit, a fantasy. It only takes one stolen dawn while all the world's asleep for the prisoner of dull routine to count himself quite free. It does not matter that the days that follow are as patterned and as uniform as the cells and chambers of a honeycomb. And so it was that father walked along the cliff-top path emboldened by the dawn and relishing the cold and deathly night he'd spent huddled by his fire.

At midday, he reached the low coast, the juice-red rocks, the overhang of salty heath where he had sheltered from the rain. Again there was a mist. But this time he did not stand and fill his lungs with damp and heavy air and cry, Who's there? He knew. He turned his back against the sea and walked inland through the fringe of arrow grass on to the heath. Quite soon he found the smudge of smoke and heard the wolf-like barking of her dog. It was the woman who called out, Who's there? He stood a little distance from her hut and did not speak. He took the goat-skin from his shoulders and held it out. His gift. She came into the open armed with a stick, the baby in a leather sling, the dog held by its neck. What she saw there was a young man in silhouette, standing on the spot where many men, on horseback, drunk, defiant, shy, had stood before, awaiting her and holding chickens, honey, cloth as payment for her time.

"Wait there," she said. She took the baby and the dog back into her hut. And then came out, untying as she walked the strings and laces which secured her winter clothes. Her eyes were on the goat-skin not the man. She'd use it as a cover for her daughter's bed.

"That'll do," she said. And then, "Lay it down. We'll

use it as a mat. The ground is wet . . ." And then, in tones that matched the pallor on my father's face, "It's you!"

If my father was in a mood for teasing he'd entertain us at this fork in his narration with a treatise on temptation. "Life is a double-headed worm," he'd say. "It can wriggle either way. It has the choice. My choice was this: to give the goat-skin as a gift, exactly as I'd meant. Or to trade the goat-skin there and then, with her, upon the ground." His audience, of course, would want the second of the two, the choice which would place my father's hands upon her waist, her hem tugged high. They'd opt for barter, fair exchange – his skin of goat, her hardly-breasts, her punctured water-bags of thighs, her patch of black, untended hair.

And then? Could he then join her in the hut and tend the pot and rock the child? Did merchants on the market green invite their clients home once all the trade was done? No, no. The pleasantries of commerce do not outlive the moment of exchange. If father had sunk down with her then their passions would be spent for good; client, merchant, interchange. She'd take the goat-skin to the child, without a word. He'd set off home with only breathlessness and muddy knees to show for all his efforts. You'd think it was an easy choice. But father – sweating, blushing, tempted, shy – could hardly speak.

The woman was looking closely at him now.

"What have you done?" she asked. "Your hair!" She reached forward and pushed her hand across his forehead and his skull. "Who's done that to you?"

"I did it to myself," he said. "To light a fire. I had no moss. I just had hair." He twisted a skein of hair between his fingers to show what he had done. "Here, I brought this skin."

"For what?"

"For you. A gift."

The dog was barking now, and the baby mewling like a gull. My father and the woman walked back to the hut with nothing dealt and everything to trade.

16

THE FIRST THING THAT MY father noticed was the stench. The saltland heath – sodden and yellowed by the winter – was sweating in the sun. It smelled like rotten fruit, like beer, like cow's breath. The earth was passing wind; it belched at every footfall; its boil had burst; it was brackish and spongy with sap and pus and marsh. And then he saw new people in the distance, their makeshift shelters, and their fires. Last year, at summer's end, there had been none – just her, the dog, the child. The heath was home to six or seven families now.

"They're waiting for the geese," the woman said. "I'm waiting, too. They come back every year, the geese, those people there. It means that summer's come. We'll eat fresh food again. I'm sick of nuts and crabs."

Once more she was obsessed with food. Goose eggs, goose fat, goose meat. She talked about the feast that there would be once the geese came in. Mesmerized, she said, by the ripe and rotten odour of the springtime heath and lured by choruses of frogs, the birds would plummet from the sky. The males would fly in first to squabble over nests and to preen themselves in readiness for mating. Then – two, three days later – the females would arrive. There'd be the rough-and-tumble of feeding, breeding, rearing young, and then, before the shortest day, the tribe of geese would rise again, their goslings too, and fly away, inland. Where to? The woman did not know. Nor could she solve the mystery of where the geese flew from, nor what there was beyond the sea, nor why the birds were not like sheep, homelovers, fearful of the outside world, faint-hearted, calm.

"Those men and women think," she said, pointing at her springtime neighbours on the heath, "that geese are people that have died. They say my husband and my boys are geese." She shrugged. "Who knows? I've also heard them say that geese bring babies, that geese bring dreams, that geese are blessings to the poor. I've heard it all. Myself, I know the truth. I've seen it every year. The geese bring summer and take away the frosts. You'll see."

The spring was early but the geese were not. My father waited for three days before the first skein passed overhead and went inland.

"Those aren't ours," the woman said. They waited three days more and, finally, at dawn, an arrow-head of geese came in from off the sea, chuckling amongst themselves and calling ahead to the people there – cowl-yar cowl-yar – that winter had pulled up its roots and fled.

My father stood and watched their flight, the nomads on the wing. They were the great pea geese. He'd seen a stray before, a single bird, exhausted, blown off course by starvation and by storms. It had fallen – just as the woman had described – onto the causeway of his village, by the market-green. No one had known quite what to do – until a stoneworker had strode from his workplace and struck the goose across the head with a wooden mallet. Then everybody knew what next. Goose meat was such a treat. They'd cooked it there and then. Its flesh was drenched and tasteless from the flight.

But he had never seen such a buoyant, stately fleet of birds before, not in such numbers, not in such rhythmic unison. He looked up at their heavy breasts, their long necks and at the slow and ponderous greeting of their wings which seemed too brief and effortless to keep such heavy birds aloft. They passed across the elderberry rocks so low that a man on horseback could have picked them from the sky like pears. And then they rose a little on the heath, repulsed it seemed by the pungency that they encountered – re-encountered – there. This was their annual resting-place. A single, leading goose swooped down like a hawk, its wings half-folded, its body dropping in a whiffling spiral dive. And soon its companions had spiralled, too, and dropped exhausted on the heath like pigeons hit by stones. Already there were other arrow-heards spread out above the sea and soon the pungent heath was throbbing, panting, with the brief distress of voyagers whose voyage now was done.

"Go on," she said. "Catch us a goose." She handed him a heavy, knuckled stick. "They won't taste at their best until they've fed. But I can't wait. Just the thought of goose is making soup inside my mouth. Go on, go on. Pick something plump."

My father had not killed before. His village had been fed by trade, not harvesting or slaughter. Already several neighbours were walking with their sticks down to the weary geese. My father followed them. He'd watch and learn their craft.

The geese were tired – but they were not entirely senseless. They understood the purpose of this human delegation armed with sticks. They scattered. They lowered their heads and necks and hissed if anyone came close. The trick, it seemed, was to stand quite still and wait. Goose-brained is what the villagers called a man whose memory was poor. There was good cause. These geese forgot the danger of the sticks once there was no noise or movement. They shuffled back to graze the grass and reeds at the butchers' feet. Six or seven paid the price. One clout across the shoulders was the best. Their weaving bodies – so sinuous and subtle on the wing – were dumplings on the heath. Killing those few was simple. It took no skill. My father stood stone-still. Quite soon he had a trusting congregation of grazing geese. He chose the plumpest, took one deep breath and grasped his stick.

Of course my father could not allow his butchery to be a speedy, plain affair. One blow, one goose, one feast. He could not – at least, in his retelling of that day – resist the role of the buffoon. "That wretched dog of hers," he said. The dog, it seemed, was just as keen as all the people there for goose. It had sunk down, its nose far-stretched, its tail tucked in, and followed father across the heath. It had found a spot in thigh-length grass where, out of sight, it could come close to father and his congregation. It took the lifting of the stick as some command. It came out of the grass with the speed and manners of a thunderclap. Its single bark sent every goose haywire. Save one. The plumpest in the congregation. It seized the bird by its wing which was as inefficient as catching lobsters by their claws. The goose began to beat the heath with its free wing. My father's stick came down, and struck the dog a glancing blow across the back. It opened up its mouth and let its prey – except some feathers – go free. The goose – unable to distinguish man from dog – went for my father's legs. Its black and yellow bill was stronger than it looked. It bit. My father fell. The goose tugged on his coat and the dog – unnerved by father's blow – stood back and barked.

We would be fools to swallow such a comic tale – the dog, the stench, my father down and caked in sap and pus and marsh – but catch a goose he did. He swears to that. Perhaps the dog regained its courage and seized the bird again. Perhaps my father and his flailing stick struck lucky. Perhaps a springtime neighbour, taking pity on the one-armed clown, simply stepped across and dealt the final blow.

17

THE WOMAN SHOWED HIM HOW to pluck and draw a goose and not waste time. The feathers must be pulled soon after death, she said, before the flesh turns cold and stiffens. She started with the feathers underneath the wings, and then the down upon the breast, and then the tougher flights on wings and tail. She seemed more animated than she had ever been before, and laughing as she worked. It was the thought of father's antics on the heath. The baby and the dog seemed happy too. Her laughter touched them all.

Once all the feathers had been pulled she singed the carcass in the fire. The plucked goose-skin became a landscape cleared by flames. She laid the blackened bird upon its back and cut its pinions and its neck. Now the crop could be removed and the entrails loosened with two fingers. She cut the body between tail and vent, worked free the gizzard and drew away the giblets in one piece so that no bitterness was spilled upon the flesh. She threw the giblets to the dog. All was achieved with the focus and the craft that father recognized from men like Leaf. She'd reshaped the goose.

Next day, his stomach tight and queasy from the goose's grey and muscular flesh, my father returned to his village.

"Take them a bird," she said, smiling at the prospect of another drama on the heath; the dog, the stick, the spongy earth, the bludgeoned body of a goose, my father (tumbled like a drunk and caked in marsh) flailing with one arm. He shook his head. "Goose meat is far too good for them," he said. He had grown selfish as all men do when they discover families, homelands, of their own. His other life was not for cousins. They had their flints, their skills, their status in the market-place, the certainties of work and trade. He had the outside world, its geese, its sailing-ships, its makeshift dwellings in the wind. They'd have to do without his geese.

He took them other gifts instead, the stories that he'd found upon his way. There was the story of the talking goose. It was snow-white except for a golden bill and feet. It said . . . and here my father could devise a goose-borne message that would tease whatever audience he had assembled at his feet. There was the story of the woman and her magic dog. They lived inside a house made out of hair. The dog could cook and stitch and start a fire. The woman hunted rabbits with her mouth. There was the story of the boy who had the gift of flames. He could spit fire. Those people who stayed close to him need never fear the cold. There was the story of the stench which, bruised and angered by a traveller who had held his nose when passing, hid inside the traveller's bag and (depending on my father's mood) came out to cause all kinds of mayhem in the world.

18

THE PATTERN THAT EMERGED WAS this –
my father was two men. One was the husband-brother-son,
the clumsy, willing settler on the heath who'd turn his hand
to anything – to feeding the small child with paste from beans
and fish; to hunting mushrooms, chasing crabs; to coddling
embers in the smoke at night as the woman and her daughter
rocked and hummed themselves to sleep. This was the man
who came to love the girl and treat her as a daughter of his
own. He knew the sweet stewed-apple smell of the childish
water that she passed. He helped her understand and say her
first few words: drink, dog, no, bird, kiss, hot. He invented
faces and new sounds for her amusement.

The other man was the minstrel-king of lies, the teller of
wide tales who could not (they said) even pick his nose with
his one helpless arm. He couldn't shell an egg. Yet, with his
tongue, he could concoct from, say, geese, ships and smells,
a world more real than real.

They did not question his migrations or interrupt the
voices that seemed to summon him away every week or so.
The villagers – or those at least whose hearts were not shut
by custom and by work to father's world of fraud and flam –
could see his need for gathering more tales on their behalf.
There were none to be unearthed amongst the workshops
and flint-piles of the stoney village. The knappers had no

tales. Such diversions must be hunted in the outside world and plucked and drawn and served up to them, reshaped and heated by my father.

So the path along the clifftop, where the gulls were upside down and where newly beaten passageways edged past rocks and winkle-berry thickets, was worn wide and flat by my father's to-and-fro. He did not need the stars or luck to find his way. The path was his. He recognized each rock, each fallen tree, each brook. Here was the debris of his fire. Here the ship's sail had ducked into the waves for good. Here the dog seals came ashore to roll and grumble in the sea's white phlegm. It could be walked – at speed – in half a day. But father took his time. There was no haste. The wind was warm. And it was true – within a few days of the arrival of the geese the spring had come. The coastal path was blue and gold with buds.

At the end of spring my father set off once again to see the woman and her daughter. By now the geese had settled down. He found them grazing on the tide line or upping in the water for the eel grass there or dozing on their eggs in nests deep in the heather. The caravan of birds was quiet and fat again. The nomads were becalmed. They scarcely stirred as father took the path across the heath towards the hut of reeds.

The geese had taught the baby how to walk. She spread her legs and rocked from foot to foot. Her arms were bony wings. Her cries – cowl-yar cowl-yar – were answered by the birds. She was the largest gosling on the heath. She lifted up her arms when my father arrived. She let him pick her up and slapped his nose in greeting. She pushed her fingers in his mouth and gripped his gums and pulled. She knew his face and smell.

The dog was yapping, too, and licking father's ankles and his feet. The woman came out of the hut. She looked wellfed. She thrived on goose. Her lips were pink. There were no greying moons beneath her eyes or sores upon her face.

"That's better now," she said, pointing at his head. "You look less like a tussock." She ran her hand across his hair as if he were her child. He would have seized her by the wrist and kissed her hand except that, if he had, he would have dropped her daughter on the dog. He rubbed her ribs with his severed elbow but she did not stay close to acknowledge his embrace. She seemed unnerved. A gang of men had passed that day, she said. Thirty, forty men. With bows and sticks. Not horsemen, but on foot. They'd camped inland, beside the wood. She pointed out the braid of smoke that their three fires were plaiting in the distance. Who could they be? Now father was unnerved. He threw wet earth upon the fire. Trouble-makers looked for smoke or light. For all his gifts of lying and invention he could not concoct a tale that night that would explain the friendly purposes of men in gangs with sticks and bows. They slept without a fire and had cold dreams of trouble-making on the heath.

Their dreams came true.

But first, there was the sound of horses. And then a voice called out, a drunken voice. "Rabbit. Rabbit. Doe." The woman and my father, submerged by fear and nightmares in the hut, their chins and faces wet with goose, awoke and held their breaths. Outside there was more laughter, and then another, younger, daring voice: "Doe-doe. Sweet doe. Come out."

"I'd better go," she said. "I know these men. They mean

no harm. Here, hold the child. I'll not be long." And then, "It's just their joke. The horsemen call me Doe. They tell their women and their neighbours that they're off to catch a rabbit when, in truth, they're coming here. You see? A joke."

She went outside, untying all her strings and laces as she walked. She held my father's goat-skin gift under her arm. There were two horsemen there, both mounted on black mares. The older rider held his horse in check. It waited for the woman as if expecting food. The younger man – about my father's age – was too impatient to control his mount. As Doe approached, as Doe the rabbit got closer to his snare, he jumped down from the horse. "Me first," he said. The older rider turned his horse and moved away a little distance, his back turned to the woman and his friend . . . his son? . . . his nephew? . . . his young charge?

My father did not turn away. He watched. He watched the braggart youth take the woman's arm and pull her roughly to the ground, the goat-skin thrown aside. He watched him stumble to his feet a few moments later and honk his pleasure like a goose. He watched the older man take his turn with Doe as the younger horseman backed and scurried in the grass to recapture the mare which in his haste he had not bothered to secure.

"I had my hand around the baby's throat," my father said. "I'd killed a goose. I'd kill her child. And then the dog. I'd pull the whole hut down and set fire to all her world. I wished I was a horseman and a bowman then. I'd put an end to beasts like them with arrows in the heart."

That's what father said. But what he did was better suited to a one-armed man of words. He kept well back in case the horsemen saw him there. He soothed the child. He held the muzzle of the dog. He cursed the malign illogic of his own erection. He swore he'd save the woman – he'd rescue Doe from tupping for a trade.

She was no fool. She understood the hurt he felt. But finer feelings were not food. They could not kindle fires. Or warm a child. You could not make a coat from finer feelings. The men on horseback that came, once in a while, with their simple needs were worth more to her than cuckoos of my father's kind. She met my father's stare with eyes that were unabashed and unashamed. She'd taken care of two men – and been paid – in the time it took a potter to block some clay or a stoney to heat one flint. She'd made them sneeze. So what? If she had to suffer men between her legs then let the cost be theirs, poor fools. She held out the object of her trade for father to admire. It was a water pot, half full of head-spin made from grain. "Forget your troubles. Drink!' she said.

He'd drunk this headspin once before – from the leather travel-mates of horsemen, on the day they cut his arm in two. But he'd had no chance to savour it. He'd drunk too much too quickly, and then they'd struck him on the chin. He'd savoured drinker's headache, that was all, and had those bad and stoney dreams. What would his cousins think, or Leaf, if they could see him now, cross-legged and urgent in the woman's hut, with spirit rolling round his mouth and anger in his eyes? They'd wonder whether stories came from drink. Was that the trick? Was that the secret of my father's to-and-fro? His wildness and his fantasies, his enmity to stone and work, came not from devils but from drink. My father did not care. His cousins only knew what they were told. He'd keep these secrets to himself, the geese, the woman and the drink. They were the outside world.

And so the two of them were drunk, though he more drunk than her. Her stomach was more tough. Her head was strong. My father was an easy prey for the liquid in the pot. It burnt his mouth at first and made him cough. But then he learnt the trick of sipping with his tongue and letting headspin melt onto his throat like sucked ice and curl into his gut and blush into his head, his heart, his eyes. He recognized the taste from bread that had gone green. But the sweetness and the power of the drink was new. It made him sneeze and wipe his eyes and fashion from the fear of men with sticks, and his hatred for the riders, and the concord of the night, and the even, conspiratorial breathing of the dog and child, a certainty that the time had come for him to touch the woman who sat in darkness at his side. Where to begin?

If father was an amateur with drink, then he was a booby and a greenhorn when it came to touch. "Who cared for me when I was small and had no mother and no home?" my father asked, in those tearful, melting moods which came with age and illness. It was our task to answer Not a One and then to hug him while he cried. "Ah, that's the cure for all woes," he'd say. "More hugs. I had no hugs when I was small. I never learned to kiss. Imagine that! The nearest that my uncle got to loving me was his mallet on my brow." And then – his spirits rising – he'd tell some tale. Of how he learned to kiss, from seal pups on the beach. Or how he learned to hug, from bears. He made a bitter joke of it, but we could tell that there was bone beneath the flesh. He ached for touch. And so he ached for her, the woman on the heath, the thin and bony widow who bartered her own flesh.

He passed the pot of headspin and, when she took it, dropped his hand on to her knee as if by chance. He said, "You're cold." And then, "What can I do to keep you warm?"

"Go out and light the fire," she said.

"But there are men out there."

"So what?" The drink had made her hard. "There are always men out there. Why should I go cold?"

"You won't go cold," he said with that breathless tenderness that women find so insincere and wearying. "I'll keep you warm." He would have put his arm round her and hugged if he'd had an arm convenient for that. But he was sitting on the wrong side of her. His stump and her arm met, two different breeds. He turned his body to her and reached with his good arm for the hair behind her head. He put his head down on her shoulder and – almost breathless from the drink and fear and expectation – kissed her on the neck. He might as well have sat with his one arm round a tree and kissed the bark for all the interest that she showed.

"You're drunk," she said. "You'd better sleep." She pushed his head away. "Stop that." But father had her taste upon his lips, the dry and ashy flavour of her skin. He could not stop. He put his hand on to her leg and stroked her there, waiting for her Yes or the courage in his arm to touch the black and hidden thicket beneath her smock. She did not keep him waiting long. The instant that his hand found nerve enough to push her clothing back she brought the pot of headspin down upon his skull. The pot was shards. My father's head – sobered and a little bruised – was drenched in drink. His eyes were stinging. His ears were ringing to the hubbub that she made in the darkness of the hut. "Get out. Go home," she said. "You don't touch me!"

Of course, the child woke up. And screamed. The dog – so recently my father's friend – snapped and growled at father's legs. My father ran outside. His passion closed its wings and plummeted in a whiffling, spiral dive. He did not move. He was a stone. He heard her cursing to herself. He heard the sweep and slap of the dog's tail. He heard the baby whimper on the breast, then sleep. All that was left was darkness, the spring wind off the sea, the guroo-guroo of night-time geese, the distant, crackling fires of strangers on the heath. My father took deep breaths. His muscles tightened with the thought of killing her. His eyes were wet – with drink and tears and cold. He wished he was a horseman now with a fist like stone and a face like weathered bark. She'd love him then, for sure.

He could not guess how long he waited. Not long – but long enough for his skin to peg and button like a goose. He did not hanker now for her caresses or her love. He wanted only to win from her some recompense. He was the story-teller, don't forget. He knew how to deepen any plot. And so he whispered in the night, his voice unsteady, wheedling, sly.

"Rabbit. Rabbit. Doe. Sweet Doe. Come out." She came at once. She stood outside her door, a still black shape. He could not guess her mood.

"I thought that we were friends," my father said.

"What kind of friend are you?" Her voice was angry still. "You think I want that kind of friend? I've plenty of that kind. They don't come in my hut. But you I've treated as a brother and a son."

"You go with all those horsemen. Why not me?"

"They pay. That's why."

"I'll pay."

She held her hand out to her brother-son. "Come in," she said. "We'll talk."

Who tells the truth about such things? Only crones and fools. My father's version went like this: The woman, Doe, was sobered by remorse. The one-armed man who'd killed the goose and brought the goat-skin gift and courted her was cold and drenched in drink and bruised about the head. She loosened all her strings and laces and at last paid back the kisses which he had invested on her neck. He'd leave it there. Such stories are best obscured by mist. The only details were the jokes at his or her expense. "You need two arms when you're on top," he'd say, a clown who knew no shame. He'd demonstrate his lopsided, toppling passion on that night. He'd shudder, too, to mime the moment when, at last, his body emptied all its seed in Doe. And then the song he sang was this: How sad is he who has no wife. His seed is trapped. It turns to poison in his loins. His blood runs hot and burns. It dries his body and he leads a pale and angry life. But he who has a woman at his side? He is as carefree as an insect on the wing.

My father flapped his one good and his broken wing to illustrate the joy he felt the moment that he, with Doe, discharged the poison in his loins, the moment when the chrysalis of lust became the butterfly. "I felt nimble. I felt light," he said, dancing to the words. "Any man will say that sneezing in the night like that will bring good sleep. And when you wake, where is the fury and the sadness and the madness that you felt? All gone. The butterfly has flown."

The truth, of course, is short of butterflies. We can presume, from what my father said on those few and candid times when we were on our own, that Doe and he remained good friends, and nothing more. When he returned to talk with her inside the hut the moment of affection was long past. The child was nervous in her sleep and stirring with bad dreams. The dog was wide-awake and alert for signs that would require more barking and more bites. There were still men in gangs with sticks and bows upon the heath. The only kisses that would be given freely in that hut would be for her daughter's lips, not his.

Although my father knew that if some horsemen came, right then, and called to her, she'd go to them – at once – he also recognized the force of what she'd said, "You don't touch me! You think I want that kind of friend? I've plenty of that kind." He did not try again to put his hand upon her knee. Besides, the wind was driving back the stars and it was nearly dawn.

She'd said, Let's talk. But Sleep is what she meant. My father did not sleep for long. He woke unsettled, mystified. The wind was racing now, the sort of wind that lifted slates from walls and sent Leaf's hair on streaming errands from his head, the sort of wind that called, "Go home, go home. To your house and stone. Go home." The mist was low and moist and chasing inland with the wind. There was no sea. My father had some business to conclude. He went outside, the dog his one companion, and discharged his poison on to the buds and seedlings of the heath. It gathered, rolled and spongy, in the dew and hung in stringy tresses from the reeds. It formed its salty pools of sap amongst the vented lichens and the moss. My father – his one hand plenty for the task – was briefly lost amongst the ardours and the lecheries of a story of his own invention. The only sounds were the pantings of the man and dog and the bickerings of geese.

19

DOE AND HER DAUGHTER WERE standing hand in hand, the child's tiny arm a twig in Doe's strong grip. My father rubbed his head to remind her of the night just past. But he had left the giblets of his lust for her hung up, like a screech owl's breakfast, on the grasses and the reeds. He was entirely calm. He bent and kissed the child.

"I could not sleep," he said. "I went down to the shore . . ." He would have entertained her with a greater lie. But, here, the dog began to whine and point its nose towards the distant wood. There were no braids of smoke. The gang of men who had slept there had spread themselves out in a line. Their bows were ready. Their sticks were out. They did not talk. They were advancing across the heath like heavy-shouldered wolves who've traced the scent of deer. The dog began to bark. It was too late to strap its jaw. It was too late to flee. The loop of men was tightening round the heath. My father, Doe, the girl, were minnows in their net.

My father – poison all discharged – was not the reckless sort. What was the point in hiding in the hut? Or looking for a stick? He might just as well throw pebbles at the tide. Whatever mayhem was in stock that day would come and go whatever father did. And so they simply stood their ground, the perfect family of the heath – my father, one-armed, a damson bruise upon his head; the woman with her daughter on her hip and her free hand resting on my father's shoulder; the dog; their frail and reedy hut. Some way off, the wasted semen had thickened and was tacky in the wind.

It soon was clear what it was the men had come to do. The first goose that they found was struck across its spine. The eggs which it had risen to protect were smashed with sticks and feet. Its nest was kicked into the wind. The grazing birds that rose to flee were greeted in the air by flights of wooden darts. They fell like pears. Their carcasses were left. These thirty, forty men were not hunting for the meat. They came to fight a war against the nomad raiders from the sea.

At first their killing was quite calm because the birds themselves were quiet and slow to leave their eggs. The hissing, flapping geese that had quickly understood the purpose of a human delegation armed with sticks on that spring day when father was the hunter had been reduced by the observances of parenthood to docile innocents. It was not hard to lift a stick and break a goose's back when the victim simply sat and made threats and patterns with its head. But once the men had finished with the outskirts of the flock, the absent males – alarmed by the keenings of their mates – flew in from their browsings and their uppings on the shore to stand and honk beside their nests. Some were brought down by darts before they had a chance to reach their eggs. The wooden shafts were not strong or swift enough to kill. But they could wound – and wounded geese are giddy imbeciles. The more they bleed, the more they flap like moths in fires, the more they stretch and weave their necks and shriek their plaints. Others – addled by the carnage and the noise – put down in territory not their own. They ducked their heads and spread their wings; they barked as dogs and gallivanted on the heath like headless hens. Of all the thousand geese upon the heath there was not one, except the dead or those in shells, which remained still or quiet or simply thought to leave its nest and fly away to sea.

By now the bows had done their work and the men were labouring with sticks. They whirled and struck like flail-dancers at a feast, every loop and detour of their steps ended with the carcass of a goose. They lifted and they stamped their feet like men in snow – except this snow was stained and creamy eggs, and its slush was yolk. The few who had no sticks found rocks – juice-red rocks – with which to kill the birds. The rocks and skulls fell open and apart, they crumbled into shards, the elderberry of the stone soaked by the blood of geese.

The few older, greying men were calm and concentrated at their task. For all the passion that they showed they might have been up-ending mushrooms with a switch. They turned from side to side and cut a swathe of geese with faces which declared, "I've seen this all before."

The younger ones were not so calm. They matched the geese in noise and fever. They swung their sticks wildly in the air. They stumbled over geese. They fell on eggs. They celebrated every blow with cries of exhortation and of swank. The death of every goose was victory for them. And every death was fuel for that odd and deadly stew of temper which, in young men, is called exuberance and which in wolves is known as brutishness. They took no notice of the family standing there, huddled like lost sheep. But when the dog – uncertain if this was cause for celebration or for attack – jumped up and set about a goose, a man whose face had more spots than hairs, hit out. His stick caught the dog on its side.

It fell and rolled. But it did not stand again. Four men had hurried up, enraptured by the hunt. Their sticks and stones went up and down like pestles pounding corn.

Now that dogs were counted as fair game, who or what could save the hut? There were injured geese which had taken refuge on the roof. Others coveyed in the long grass at its base. Their blood was making patterns on the wall's caked mud. Some tried to burrow and escape through the bracken fronds which Doe had placed in bunches on the ground to keep out draughts and rats. The young men gathered round. Here was unexpected fun. Only a fool would – like the dog – run up to intervene. The hut collapsed onto the geese. It fell apart and splintered like an empty husk of corn.

"Let's leave." Father lifted up the girl and picked his way between the bodies of the geese. Doe faltered for a moment at the hut. What could she salvage from the wreckage there? The young men steamed and quivered with their sticks and watched her as she turned the broken shards of pots, the ripped and trampled mats, the shells and coloured stones with which her daughter had often played, the holed and ageing fish traps that her husband had once made, the carcass of her dog. They idly clapped their hands, shouted, laughed, jousted boasts about the work they'd done that day. Doe knew that they were mad like hiveless bees. One nervous move and they'd attack. The crushing of the dog and hut had made them skittish, itching for more fun, more death. Some sex. Some drink. A rape. A fight. She did not let them see her eyes or spot the tears that made a shallow, dampened delta in the crow's feet of her face. She did not speak aloud the thought that mostly bothered her, that now the geese were dead the summer would not come.

Doe followed father, empty-handed, as he walked towards the sea. Their path across the heath was marked by fleshy, bloodstained boulders, which feathered and which shivered, going hot and cold with colour as the sea wind smoothed and stirred.

An old man called out before they reached the beach. His face was as drawn and bearded as an ear of wheat. There was blood upon his legs and hands. "Here, take a goose," he said. "They're good." He mimed by chewing and by ramming fingers in his mouth. "Good meat." And then when Doe and father just walked by, he called out, "They had to die, those geese. We'd starve if they lived on."

They stood to hear his reasons for the massacre of birds. He and his friends were all plain farmers – that was his excuse. They had a village and some fields beyond the forest, less than one day's walk inland. They'd slashed and burned a clearing there about ten years before. The life was good, so far. The earth was rich. The trees cut out the wind. The pigs were fat and happy just as long as there was food and sleep. The people too. There were reeds for thatching and for bedding. There was nettle thread. And, after every gale, a glut of wood.

The old man described a farming year that was as rhythmic as a drum. The first note in the spring was emmer wheat. Then six-row corn. Then beans. Then flax, the last to bed, the hater of the frost. The goats did well all year on fodder mulched from leaves. Their milk and cheese were said to taste of elm or ash depending on the forest where they fed. In autumn there were unearned gifts in mushrooms, nuts and fruit. In winter there were bacon sides and apples wrinkled like a widow's cheek, and grain from rat-free, stilted stacks.

There was a field of fat-hen, too. Each dark and fleshy leaf was cussed like a nostril hair. Each one removed would grow again with doubled strength. The new leaves, stewed, were vegetables. The old ones – picked and dried and stacked like hay – were winter feed for beasts. The fat-hen seeds made fat-hen bread. The roots made beer. Nothing went to waste. Even dead fat-hen was good as kindling for the fire.

The farmers were not rich, of course, or powerful or satisfied. There were hard times. Who could predict the rain? Or the mood of horsemen passing by? Or the vagaries of pigs? Who could ever win the war against the charlock and the couch which were the stifling siblings of their crops? But, for all their curses and their woes, their cheeks were fat, their skins were clear, their guts were tenanted throughout the year with food. Until the geese put down, that is, until the geese discovered that cultivated fields were better than the heath, once eggs were hatched and summer come and goslings trained to fly.

At first the farmers had been pleased to welcome the few geese who came to browse between the rows of fat-hen and of wheat. Goose meat was richer than smoked pork. Goose fat was good for piles. The gosling feathers made pillows which, despite the stench, were softer and more warm than straw. Besides, the geese were cheerful birds. Their calls were melodies compared to conversations held by pigs and goats. Their coats were brighter, too. But then – two years before – the nomads had arrived in strength, their numbers doubled by the young who'd hatched upon the salty heath. They'd harvested the field, these airborne slugs. They'd cropped the emmer and the beans, the fat-hen and the six-row corn. They'd coppiced charlock to the root. And then flown off, inland. They'd done the same the following year. And worse. They'd fouled the pasture. Their green and curly droppings had burned the soil, had overloaded loam with dung, had tainted all the earth. The farmers had no choice. They'd go to war against the caravan of birds. They'd arm themselves with sticks and bows. They'd march down to the heath. They'd show the wild world who was king by wiping out all geese.

20

"IMAGINE THIS," MY FATHER SAID, reconstructing their dilemma. They had no home. There were a thousand dead geese on the heath. Already flies were sated on the blood. And beetles, ants and slugs were searching for a passage through the feathers. The sky – which so recently had been ruffled only by the wind – was bringing in the ravens and the crows. Magpies were feasting on goose eyes, and crabs were straying from the shore, bedevilled and seduced by meat. "No one knows where maggots live," he said. "They cannot fly or swim. But maggots crawled and tumbled in the guts of geese before the birds were cold." All this before the wolves arrived and plunged their noses into the moist and pungent dead. All this before the blood enriched the soil and toadstools flourished there and carcass shrubs trailed blossoms on the sinew and the bones.

The farmers had gone home to feast on their achievements. If they'd stayed, my father claimed, they would've seen precisely who was king of that wild world. "When everybody's dead, there'll still be crabs and flies and carcass shrubs and weeds to strip and clothe the world. There'll still be stone."

So it seemed to him, the knapper's son, as he stood with Doe in the carnage of the heath and listened to the old man talk of husbandry, that the world was cut in two – one for chaos, one for coma – just as the scriptures of his village said. All the outside world required was the liberty to pound and crush, to hammer and to bruise. It didn't matter what. It didn't matter if the blows were rained on geese or huts or dogs or boys, so long as there were blows and careless brawls and sudden gusts of hardship to blow good fortune down.

At home – that other, duller world, where now my father steered Doe and her daughter to start their lives afresh – the village blows were innocuous and prescribed. They were rained down on flint. He . . . they, the workers with two hands, were made tame, secure and virtuous by labour. Their skill was their salvation and their numbness. For once the village of my father's birth, contemplated from that battlefield of geese, seemed – what was his phrase? – as snug as poppy seeds. Such was the gift of stones.

21

PERHAPS NOW IS THE TIME to make myself quite clearly known to you. It will not do if I stand darkly by to cough and comment at my father's tale. It is my story, too, and I should show my face. You know me as my father's daughter and his only child. All that is false. His title "father" was well earned, though not by right of blood. We are not kin.

I am the girl of Doe.

I am the child that he first touched when mother said "Please help". She left him standing there, in charge of chicken, dog and child, his gift of samphire fallen at his feet, while she walked off to greet the horseman on the heath. I was the child he rocked to sleep or fed with bean paste and with fish, the one with whom he practised early words like drink and dog and bird. It was for my amusement that he perfected his repertoire of faces and new sounds. I was the first in his adult, one-armed life to barter love with love. So father he became. So father he remains for me.

It was on my father's arm, with my mother, Doe, exhausted by the slaughter of the geese and the walk along the coast, trailing in our wake, that I first came upon the villagers of stone. My age was not yet two, yet I maintain that I recall that day. We were walking with our backs against the wind and sea. The path was springy, bracken. It led up from the crusty boulders of the shore to the windy brow where Leaf had built his huts. His walls were thick and packed with moss. There was no sign of life – except that, tapping in the wind, there was the rhythmic beat of antler tine on flint, the squeak of bellows, the hum of people hard at work.

Once we had walked beyond the brow and the wind had dropped we heard those beats and taps, those hums and squeaks, in jostling profusion. They sounded like the first and heavy drops of summer rain or like a thousand nutbirds pecking at a shell. The further that we walked into the village, the heavier the rain of pecks, the quieter the sea and wind, the more uniform and tended the walls and pathways that we passed. It must have seemed, to one so young and sensuous as me, that we had sunk into a dream where all disorder had been vanquished by invisible and systematic hands. Compared to what we'd left behind, the turmoil and the passion of the heath, here was a world of symmetry and of composure.

Quite soon we heard the sound of voices. The merchants were at work. We came on to the market-green and there – amongst the produce and the crowd – my father saw his uncle trading stone. Now my recollections become enmeshed in father's version of that day. How many times since then I've watched him mime his uncle's face, its irritation and dismay, its comic fear of our fatigue and what it meant, as we approached his trading-stall. We looked to him for heat and food and sleep. He looked at us as if we were weevils in his bread. He had no choice – in front of all his neighbours and the purchasers of stone – but to welcome father and his family home.

22

THAT EVENING UNCLE ASKED MY father to explain. There was no point in telling lies, my father said. If what he wanted was a woman for a tale, he'd not invent one quite like Doe. There she was, reduced and tearful in their midst. They all could see she was no siren from a ship. Her perfumes were of wood smoke and of slott. Who'd want a dab of that around their throat or wrists? Her clothes were brown and grey. Her skin was scarred and pallid, her face a mask of weariness from all the weeping and the walking that she'd done. Her eyes – quite clear and grey and unabashed when she and father had first met – were, in a single glance, both hard and meek. Was she the only story he'd brought home? His cousins were not pleased, though knowing him, they waited for the twist. "Why have you brought her here?" they asked. "What use is she to us? What can she do? Whose is the girl? Not yours, for sure. She's got too many arms."

Listen now. I'll tell you what my father said. It was dusk outside his uncle's house. The uncle's cronies were all there, the cousins and some merchants, Leaf, some knappers who had left their workshop and its shadows to walk and cough up chalk into the air. Say twenty men, some wives, some boys, a dog, a hen, the first of night-time's bats and moths, the moon. Father's returns to the village always gathered crowds. His stories were – like rare and distant perfumes, cloths and jewels – much prized.

"You see I have a woman here," he said, indicating where my mother sat and dozed on the outskirts of the crowd. "A small girl, too. Shhh, let them sleep because what I have to say is meant for you, not her." That sent a wave of interest through the people gathered there. What they expected was some fun, some bloated indiscretions or some jokes at her expense. He raised one hand and wagged a finger. Be quiet, be still, it said.

"This is a story made by life," he said. "It's true in every way." That caused some cautious laughter and some shouts. "You know that when I want to make your eyes stretch wide, I stretch my stories wide to match. You know that when I want some fun, I let my stories tickle truth. You know all that. You are not fools. Well, now, here is a tale that's meant to make you weep. There is no need for camouflage. The world out there is sad enough. So this is not a dream. This, to a hair, is fact." He'd never heard an audience so quiet. They sat and waited to be entertained by truth.

It was a love story of a sort. The girl was pretty with grey eyes. No man could pass her by without blushing at the courage of her gaze. When she was young she met a man who lived close by. Their parents were at war. Some ageing insult was roosting in the trees between their homes. They would not speak. They would not let the daughter see the son. And so the lovers ran away. Why not? Chance is a pear. It isn't ripe for long. It drops. It rolls away. It rots.

Where did they run? Not far. The man knew of a heath where they could live quite well. The sea was close, with fish and crabs and laver and marshy beds of samphire, too. If she liked rabbits, he'd trap them for her. They'd eat well. And, in the spring, the wind would bring in geese. Had she never tasted goose eggs, or its flesh? Then she would. He took her to a hide which had been built upon the heath when last spring's geese had arrived late and the people waiting there had grown cold. It was the summer and quite warm. The sea and sky were matching blues. The earth was dry and firm. The man caught fish and gathered samphire. They grilled the fish on hot, red stones which crumbled in the fire. They stewed the samphire in sea water. She watched him as he stripped the flesh with his front teeth and threw the stem into the fire. She did the same. Their stems embraced. They whined and bubbled in the fire like spit in love. That night – and here my father's neighbours held their breath – they lay together on beds of rush. They talked – then dreamed – of what it would mean to live their lives in pairs.

They had two boys. There were no problems with the births. They all grew strong on mussels roasted in hot stones, on baked guillemot, on lobsters, coalfish, kale. If there was any food to spare, or if the reeds were long enough to pull, or if the rabbit-traps were generous, then the man would take them for exchange at the villages close by. He'd bring back milk and cheese and beans. And beer. One day he bartered a basketful of laver for a pup. It was the litter runt of hunting dogs. He gave it to the boys. They had a dog and food and fun. They felt as if their heath was blessed. Even the wind, it seemed, which came in steady from the sea was whistling their tune.

"That chit who's sleeping there," my father said, pointing at poor Doe, "was once as serene and fleshy as a seal." The circle turned and looked – or tried to look because the dusk was down and, for all they knew, the woman and her girl were gone. But – with my father's help – they remembered her, the thinness of the skin and hair across her skull, the jackdaw shoulders, the insect hands. You know the story-teller's tricks; with every detail in the list he mimed and had some fun with jackdaws, insects, skulls.

The task he'd given them was this: transform that woman's carcass into seal. The stoneys and the merchants there were happy to oblige. They'd had an irksome day. Their heads had been in cages since sallow dawn. Their eyes had been fixed on stones and on their merchandise. Constructing seals from bones brought puckers to their noses, eyes and mouths. They saw her there, a sea-going slug upon the beach, weighed down by flesh and happiness.

Now they were ready for the whale. This was the rorqual that the sea had washed onto the red and juicy rocks. The tide backed off. The creature drowned on air. The boys – by now they were the masters of the heath – had never seen a whale before except as spray offshore. This one was twelve men long. Its belly and its chest was bright and fissured like a silver birch. Its back was ash. Quite soon these trunks were red with fruit where the seagulls had pecked holes.

Doe, her husband and the dog came down with knives. The tide, the night – and seagulls – left them little time. Already they could hear the wolves calling out their bids for meat. The crabs were massing too. Again my father had some fun with seagulls, crabs and wolves. His audience was beached and left helpless by the warp of words, the weft of mime, in father's storytelling net.

"The man soon showed his boys how whales were cut," my father said. "They had sharp knives. The best. Let's not waste good blushes in the dark by saying where that village was that mined and worked these knives." He pointed at his severed arm. "Let's simply say that these were tools well used to cutting flesh." He held up his hand and formed a perfect, leaf-shaped knife as thin as air. He mimed the body of the whale. He was its weight, or so it seemed. He showed exactly what it took to cut into the silver-birch bark of the belly, how meat was carved away in cubes, how skin was stripped, how candle-fat was melted into scallop shells with reeds as wick. He showed how hard it was for two adults and two boys to snap the rib bones from the whale. They stood upon each rib as if it were a bouncy bough. They jumped in unison until the rib detached, and then they tumbled with it onto the shore, the dog and seagulls squabbling for the jelly and the blood.

Quite soon they had enough long bones and meat and fat and skin. In the morning they would go to the market-green. They'd do good trade. Each rib was worth a horse, or a cow, or a pair of goats. Four ribs could make a hut. One rib would keep a carver prosperous and busy for a year. One tiny piece of rib would make a needle of such sharpness that it would never dull. Thank fortune for the sea, the tide, the wind. It had brought the whale ashore. The whale would make them safe and rich.

It was no wonder, father said, that they were reckless on that night. "The boys were fast asleep. You know the world. The woman and her man embraced. They didn't take much care." He let that last phrase tease a little in the night. And then, "The careless lovers are the ones with memories in flesh, a baby on the hip, one on the breast, one waiting to be served, one on its knees, another with its finger in the food, two others fighting on the ground, three dead and buried, and a dozen more to come. The careful lovers are the ones who . . . let's not say what. There are a thousand ways. But here's a tip from me. You know the oarweed on the shore? It's just the thing and just the size. It's smooth and wet and opens like a pouch. You put it on. I'll not mime that. But, men, watch out for crabs. And women, eels."

The guffaws that my father earned with such fantasies as this were as hollow as a wormed-out nut. No one knew for sure if father was sincere. His oarweed tip had all the style of truth but all the signs of foolery as well. Who would be the first one there to try it out? Which father, lover, beset by babies and by lust, would pioneer the oarweed harvest on the shore? What price would every neighbour pay to be a moth upon the wall when that first man, bedecked in weed and naked, talked sweetly to his smiling wife?

My father clapped his hands to bring them back. It was too dark to see him wink. "Remember who this story's for," he said. "We have two lovers rich with whale. They could afford another child to add to their two boys. That night – as scavengers wrestled on the beach for food – they wrestled on their mat. He did not let her simmer there while he ran down to rummage amongst the wolves and crabs and gulls for oarweed on the shore. Life's far too short for that. They were in love. That night his seed broke from its husk. It put out shoots. It put out roots. A girl was made. That girl who's sleeping with her mother there. You see, I tell no lies. She's there, she's there, if you could only see her through the dark. She's flesh and blood and bone. Shhh, let her sleep. This story is too sad for her."

At dawn, my father said, they loaded up a sled with

whale and tied on the ribs. The man, the boys, the dog set off towards the village where the stoneys lived and where the richest market was. The journey would take all day. One day for trade. Another day to get back home. Three days in all. The woman was content. In three days' time they would have livestock of their own. Fresh goat's milk, that was the summit of her ambition. She'd be fulfilled. Except that her husband and her boys – my true father and my brothers – did not come home. The dog came back, unscathed. But no one else.

Who knows what happened in those days, my new-found, story-telling father asked his cousins. No one will ever know. Perhaps they perished amongst the knappers here. Perhaps Doe's husband thought like this: I have my sons and all this wealth in bones upon my sled. I'll find myself a younger wife and a home less windy than the heath.

Perhaps they met with wolves, attracted and made cruel by the smell of dog and whale. The dog ran off. The man and boys were too entwined with the riches on the sled. They did not run. They died.

Perhaps they were abducted by the trees at night. They strayed into the breathing forest. The roots sprang from the soil and held the boys. A branch curled round their father and held him tight, so that he could not scream or use his fists and feet. The dog barked at the trees and showed its teeth, and then turned tail and fled the forest. In time the bodies of the man and boys turned to wood. Their skin was bark. Their eyes were knots. Their arms were boughs. Their blood was sap. Any travellers who passed by there would get to know the trees whose knobs and trunks were men, whose roots were swollen in the shape of boys. Those trees were signposts through the wood.

Or, perhaps, the truth was this. A pair of horsemen were camped along the way. They'd trapped two rabbits with a snare. They'd eaten rabbit for three days. They were eager for a change. Such was their luck that here was whale meat on a sled. They'd only eaten whale meat once before. They set their horses square across the path. They said, let's swap. You take the rabbits. We'll have whale.

Doe's man was careful not to give offence. He offered them a generous cut of meat. But now the horsemen did not care for meat. They counted up the ribs which bounced and rattled on the sled. They knew their worth. Perhaps they bantered for a while, toying with the man's politeness and his fear. Perhaps they simply took their clubs and sticks and bartered with some bruises to his head. One thing's for sure, in transactions such as that, it is the horsemen who grow rich and not the man and boys on foot. They would have dragged the bodies into undergrowth. Perhaps they aimed some idle kicks at the dog and then left it there to lick its masters' icy cheeks. That night they'd boast of their good luck and dine on whale. Perhaps.

"What should the woman do?" my father asked. "Her husband and her boys were gone. The whale was picked and cleaned and broken up by stones and tide and washed back out to sea. If you were her, what would you do to find your family again, once you'd tired yourself with tears? If you were wise, you'd take the dog and point its nose and follow where it led. She did just that. It led her here. Of course. Where else? This was her husband's destination. Don't laugh. I've told you once before, this is a story made by life. This, to a hair, is fact. That dog came here. It brought her to the market-green. Such wealth, such homes, she thought. But the people here, they had no time for her. She had no merchandise, just tears and questions and a dog. What happened to my family here, she asked. Does anybody recognize this dog? Did anybody deal in whale and bones a little while ago? Who'll help me now? You sent her home without replies. And now she's back again, with me. Does no one recognize her face?''

Consider now the consternation that my father's story caused. He'd brought its characters to life and placed them in his uncle's house, sleeping, close enough for the villagers to hear their snores, and for their snores to sound like accusations and complaints.

Quite soon they found it far too dark and cold to listen to my father any more. They peeled away before the tale was done, unmoved by father's portrait of the widow and her child on the heath, her struggles not to die, her hardships, grief and hunger, the slaughter of the geese, the crushing of her hut. Quite soon there were no cousins left to hear my father's tale. His audience – excluding bats and moths – had crept away, unamused and angered by the venom in his voice.

My father stood alone and startled – for now he understood the power of the truth.

23

NOW I CAN REMEMBER FOR myself. I do not need my father's floating eyebrow or his single, restless hand or the baiting and dramatic contours of his voice to shape and ornament my life. I do not need his hawks for commentary. I have my own.

My witness-hawk took wing when I was two or three. Each dawn it rose above the village, my feathered memory, to hover and to scrutinize what passed for life below. I see myself, a little plainer and a little plumper than my mother ever was. I see her, too. My mother was not happy there. She had good cause. In father's boyhood there had been two breeds existing side by side, the stoneys and the mongers, the craftsman dynasties who worked the flint and the traders whom the stone made rich. My father now had introduced a third and wretched breed, the pair of homeless vagrants from the heath. What could we do?

At first we simply shivered to the welcome that the villagers gave us. Their indifference was prying. There were no greetings, but they raised their eyes as we walked by and paused above their stones. They clearly disapproved. Of what? Our meagre clothes, our weathered skin, our helplessness, our voices which – more used to shouting in the wind than trading whispers by the hearth – were loud? Here were people with the eye to penetrate a stone, to look beyond the crust of smoky, mottled chalk and spy the tool within. Yet that eye was blind if required to pierce a stranger's skin, to judge a woman by her face, to spot the empty stomachs and the empty hearts which could be filled and warmed as much by smiles as food.

My father said that they were shy, suspicious, that they were only used to dealing with new faces over trade. "It will take time," he said.

"It will take time for them to change? Or us?" my mother asked. She was dismayed at everything she saw, and father took the blame. She had no wish to be like them, tied and bound by the regulation of the working day. What kind of life was that? To live like tethered goats in one small sphere of grass; to do and say exactly as the neighbours; to not touch this or that, to not go here or there; to intervene all day between your heart and tongue; to turn out, at dawn, and climb the flint-pit hill in listless, yawning lines because some merchant had the force to say, More Stone.

Still, we had to stay.

"There is no choice," my father said. "We'll have to make here home." But making homes was not his skill. The one-armed man who seemed to manage on the heath was here – a cousin's phrase – just like a cuckoo, good at Talk, not Do. For all his plots and promises he could not build four walls of stone, a roof, a house. He could not lift with his one hand. My mother could. Despite her paleness and the shallow flesh that hid her bones, she was tough. And tougher here, with people all around, than she had been upon the heath, disarmed and addled by her widowhood.

My father's plot was this – that Doe and I were now his family; that we would settle into love, with Doe his sister, mistress, friend entwined with him; that, given time, his uncle and his cousins would provide. He thought his tongue would build a home for us.

My mother's toughness was an axe that had two blades. Its second edge was petulance. She could not wait for father to conjure up stone walls. Her back was cold. She had a child to feed. She had no time for father's fondness, his clumsiness, his tales. She found his presence irksome. She pushed him far away because she was too overwhelmed by cares for gentleness. All she yearned for was a home that could not be broken down with sticks.

And so, while father went hunting with his toes for shellfish in the sand and wondered whether the water in his eyes was spray or tears, Doe cleared a site of bracken in between the last house of the village and the hill. This was the spot where the many clifftop paths converged into one steep track and passed between the two rock sentries to climb the bluff of chalk and reach the warren of mine shafts beyond and the drifts of unworked flint. She was no fool. It was a simple task to find flat building stones amongst the spoils and then to slide them downhill from the summit of the track until they settled on her bruised and flattened bracken.

The hill was on her side. The villagers were not. She could not hope to help herself to stone without some stoney raising the alarm. A delegation came of busybodies and of idlers. They pushed Leaf to the front and whispered what they'd want to say if they were him. Leaf was not pleased to be summoned from his work to deal with such affairs. The wind was lifting all his hairs and making knots. My mother met him with a look that said, You're less than geese. You don't scare me.

"These stones are ours," he said. "Who said that you could take these stones?"

"These stones are mine," she said. "I found them on the hill. I brought them here. They're mine. How are they yours?"

"You're not from here. That hill is ours, not yours."

"And the air round here is yours as well," she said. "I breathe; I steal your air. And the wind that's making such a skimpy harvest on your head? Is that your wind? How can it be that it blows my hair, too?"

Leaf was not equipped for Doe. He shrugged and cursed the wind.

"We'll let these stones be gifts from us," he said. "But do not fool yourself. That hill is ours. If you take stone, what then? Then anyone can come and help themselves and build a wall. But still, you are a woman with a child. We'll close our eyes on you and what you do." He turned and led his delegation back to work. My mother built her walls.

24

OUR HOUSE WAS LIKE NO other. My mother found that stones, however flat and heavy, were not keen to lie still at her bidding. Her stones were like the shyest snails which never showed their heads, but moved when no one watched. Her stones had life. They crept. They nestled. They muttered in the wind and heat. And so she built four living walls which would not stand like all those other village walls made out of more quiescent stones. Her walls were wayward, unsubmissive. They toppled in the wind. They barked her ankles. They fell down on my leg and did not move despite my screams and tears.

She could not guess the secret of a wall. Her walls became four piles of stones, thick at the ground and tapering like sapling firs. She pushed lengths of wood between the stones to keep them still. She packed the holes with bracken and with mud. The roof was untrimmed branches weighed down with slates and moss. Our house was what a house would be if it were made for badgers or for bears.

At first, our lives were like theirs too, furtive, taciturn, aloof. If father was two men then mother was two women. The village Doe was wary of the world. If stoneys passed we sank into our cave. If father came with food, my mother would not talk. Her temper was as chronic as the wind – and just as indiscriminate.

What explanation can there be for my mother's sudden, random sourness? It's just that people are like trees. They have their seasons, too. They don't transplant. For Doe, my father was to blame for all the bad luck in her life. Who else was there – apart from me – who could share the burden of her dislocation and her grief? That small voice which whispered at her cheek and said, Be rational. Return his love. Accept his food. He's all you've got, was silenced by the volume and the force of her despondency. The louder voices cried, What kind of friend is he? He'd led her from the mayhem of the geese along the coastal path with promises of food and shelter and of warmth. What welcome had there been? – Why have you brought her here? What can she do? What use is she to us?

She could not forget that first and bitter night when she had listened, only half-asleep, to what my father had to say to his assembled cousins and their friends in the dusk of uncle's house. "This is a story made by life," he'd said, and then produced a tale so close to truth that she'd believed his ornamented details, too, the insult roosting in the trees, the spitting samphire meal, the serene and fleshy portrait of her younger self, the bouncing family on the rorqual bones, the oarweed on the shore. She'd swallowed that. It was her story, feathered and adorned.

What she was forced to swallow, too, were all the versions of her husband's death, the killing of her boys. Perhaps abducted by the trees at night? Perhaps by wolves, or horsemen? My father brought their deaths to life. He dragged their bodies into undergrowth. He turned their bodies into wood. Their arms were boughs. Their blood was sap. Their skin was bark. Their eyes were knots. And worse. He'd said: "Perhaps Doe's husband thought like this – I have my sons and all this wealth in whale. I'll find myself another wife and a home less windy than the heath.''

Consider once again the consternation that my father's story caused, not to the twenty men, the wives and boys, the dog, the hen, the moon, the first of night-time's bats and moths that had gathered there. They could simply peel away before the tale was done. Instead we should consider poor and captive Doe, the homeless widow, underfed and half-awake, her lungs so tight with fear that she was snoring open-eyed. Death she understood. It came. It went. It left a corpse. Corpses could not trade in whale. Or set up house away from wind and heath. Or take new wives. But a missing husband and two sons? My father's story – which with a string of tales, ''perhaps . . . perhaps'', had killed them off five times for good, destroying every hope she'd had – had also brought them back to life. He had them fit, and well, and dwelling – wind-free – somewhere else. With someone else.

My father had released three breeds of grief to gnaw and tumble in her gut. Her boys and husband were alive in her again and hating her for leaving home before they had returned. Or else she saw them living on the heath, the boys no older than the day they'd left – but the woman they called mother was not called Doe. Or else she saw their bodies there, amongst the geese. The trailing blossoms of the carcass shrubs were torn and buffeted by wolves and crabs and crows. The maggots rolled and tumbled like the surf. Toadstools dined on flesh. She dreamed herself back on the heath, making graves. My father was there, too. He could not help. One arm was not enough. Instead he stood a short way off, a little stunned by mother's pot and drenched in hard-earned drink. The dog and child awoke, alarmed. The heath was stirring to the cries of "Get out. Go home. You don't touch me!" And then she saw the strangers' braid of fire and heard the slap of harnesses and reins and the pestle-pounding of her dog, her hut. She built a cairn of stones above her husband's grave. The stoney with the balding head arrived. He said, "Those stones are ours, not yours."

No wonder mother could not talk to father or thank him for his gifts or show the casual openness which had ensnared him on the heath. She was a different woman now. He was a different man. The sea wind on the coastal path had turned them upside down. The truth of what she felt for him had tumbled like a ball of gorse. The one-armed lad, the brother, friend and son, who'd cheered her up so much had gone. What could she say when father stood before her house of stones, his one hand bearing comforts, clothing, food, and asked her why she looked, at once, so hard and meek and cold? What had become of the woman that he pictured on the heath?

My father's picture – naturally – was more a flight of romance. It was blind. Its centrepiece was me and Doe. She pushed her hand across his forehead and his skull. She stroked his tussock hair. In tones that matched the pallor on my father's face, she said, "It's you. It's you. It's you."

Here were two people, then, unsteady and misshapen. Their world, that summer, was as restless and as tousled as an unshorn goat. My father was the wisest of the two. For once he held his tongue. He did not bully mother to conform. He came with food and seashore gifts and left without a word to her. He carried me down to the shore and let me search and paddle in the pools. Together we collected empty shells. We wrestled and played chase. Where father failed with mother, he was bound to win with me. I had no picture of the heath and nothing to forget.

If father was the wisest one, then mother, once again, was the most determined. Quite soon she found that life for badgers and for bears was not for her. Perhaps the villagers would find a niche for her inside their world of stone.

Instead of hiding behind her tumbled walls when stoneys passed, she took to standing in their way and greeting them with cries and smiles. Her thin and bony frame was no threat to them. The village men – no paragons of strength compared to farmers, say, or horsemen – could have pushed her to one side as if she were a twig, if that is what they wished. But what they wished was something else. My mother – standing in their way, thin-set and unabashed – was a challenge of a different and uncertain kind. She was not like the mothers and the wives with whom they lived. She was not tame. Her house, her pile of stones and branches, was not a house. It was a den, an earth, a lair.

So it turned out that there were men who took the pathway in between the village and the hill more frequently than they had done before. They found good cause to walk up to the double-sentry rocks in search of flints, let's say, that normally their youngest sons could find. And if they saw that Doe was not in sight, they found excuse to whistle or to sing or drop their rocks and curse or clear their chalky chests so that the noise would summon her and she would block their path. Some stayed aloof. They'd only passed that way to pry. Some traded greetings and walked on. But there were two or three among the stoney men – the sort who were the first to make a crowd, the last to bed at night – who were less proud. There is a phrase, Whenever man and woman meet, then Mischief is the third. In this case Mischief was bashful and discreet. It hung around but it hung back. It bode its time. Those unproud men, most used to angular and patterned lives, could hardly speak their minds. What could they say? That somewhere in between the pity and disdain that they felt for mother and for me was pinched and pressed a busy hankering for mischief in the grass. For all they knew such naked words would bring the hill down on their heads. Besides, they dare not chance what mother might reply. She was the sort, it seemed, who might delight in spreading indiscretions. That was her danger and her charm.

There are old men who can remember Doe. I've heard them talk. No man would claim that she was beautiful or young or that her face was anything but dispirited and thin. Her only allure, it seemed, was her independence and defencelessness. And yet – that other phrase that seemed to rule our lives – She was Honey, They were Bees. Once they had sampled her sweet and angry greetings and her smile, so more unguarded in their manner than those that village women gave, they could no more keep away than they could openly solicit her for greater trade than smiles.

My mother was uncertain, too. Stoneys were not horsemen. Their faces were a fog. She feared their rigid, hidden lives, their mouths. She feared their coolness and their caution. The dog that does not wag its tail or bark, she told herself, is the dog to watch. It bites. So she was slow in saying what she wanted from those two, three men who'd stop and talk with her. If only she could say, Please, help me build a house that doesn't shift and groan like shingle on the beach. Or, What is there to do? What work is there for me? Then, perhaps, that niche inside the village would appear. It was a village, after all, where trade was king, where labour was respected. All my mother had to trade was labour and herself. She was just like them. She'd rather be like them than like a badger or a bear.

There was one man – my father's eldest cousin – who seemed to pass our house of stone more frequently than even those few men who talked. He was not one who simply stared and passed on by. He was prepared, if not to smile, at least to nod at Doe. Each day he came with an empty sled made out of bone and wood and reed. His task was to collect the flint for his family to work and trade. Of all the cousins he was the dullest and the most obliging. "Just like a sheep," my father said. He was the cousin that my father liked the best. He was the servile, cheerful sort, too soft and brotherly to wonder why the daily job of fetching stone was always his.

She followed him. Sometimes alone and sometimes with me sitting on her hip, she watched the cousin selecting stones and loading up the sled. She saw he favoured flints with ridges and with tendons. She watched him jettison those stones that seemed all chalk, too pale and light in colour and in weight. She noted how he piled the stones onto the sled so that their spurs and pinnacles, their bays and basins interlocked. At last she understood the secret of a wall. And more. She recognized there was no future for her there unless she became a stoney too. In such a place you earned respect through flint. It was the bedrock of their world. Without their stones the villagers would be – like her upon the heath – as helpless as a beetle on its back.

This was my mother's choice, to be the helpless beetle on its back or else the working beast obliged to gather flint because – remember her initial fears? – some merchant had the force to say, More Stone. She chose More Stone. She simply said to father's cousin when she next found him sledding flint, "Let me do that! Why don't you let me fetch the flint for you?" We can imagine how he laughed – or blushed, or walked on by. How could a woman with fir-shaped walls know anything of stone? How could a weather-beaten chit like her move heavy loads?

She might have had to pester him for days on end with "Let me try" or "I'm as strong as any man – just give me half a chance" or "Have a heart. I've got a child to feed" before he paid her any heed. And then what could this shy, obliging cousin do except allow this woman and her child to help him load the sled at least? And then to let her walk with him – taking turns at pulling on the ropes – down into the village, its empty causeways, its eyes and minds engrossed, its workshops beating with the pulse of bone on wood on stone. We have to guess that no one saw them passing by. The cousin would have shrank away in shame if anyone had called out or teased him, later, about the woman at his side.

He must have made her wait outside the house in case his family spotted her. The only way to make her go was payment of some kind, some recompense for those few flints that she had added to his pile. He could not comprehend exactly what the barter was and who owed what to whom, or why. He only understood the obligations of labour and of trade, that picking stones and pulling sled for half a noon was worth – a guess – a basketful of apples? Some grain? Some nuts? An egg or two? He felt as if he had been fooled by her. The kindness had been his. He had not wanted her to help or welcomed extra hands upon the rope. She'd merely slowed him down. Yet now it seemed he was obliged to pay for her intrusion.

There were twists of bacon drying in the smoke above the fire. He pulled one loose. It would not be missed. He went outside and, avoiding Doe's grey eyes, gave the twist to me and scuttled back to the simplicities of flint. By dealing with a child, he thought, he had sidestepped yet satisfied the rituals of exchange.

We should not laugh at his bad luck. Yet there was something lumbering and comic about the look that crossed his face when he approached the hill next day. Doe was waiting for him there, between the double guards. She called him cousin. She pointed to the pile of perfect flints that she had already chosen for his sled. Let's not call on the image of the honey and the bee. This cousin had no sting. He was a simple blow-fly caught – and flapping – in the finest web.

He thought his fortunes had improved when she seemed happy to allow him to load and take away her stone without her help. He said, "Stay here, and when I come again I'll bring another twist of bacon for the girl."

"Bring something else," my mother said. "We've meat enough for now. Bring bread. Or milk." He was happy to oblige. It was a bargain if compared to the embarrassments of yesterday. He was content to share these odd and teasing intimacies with her so long as she and he were out of sight. Besides, the flints she'd piled were good enough. Why should he complain?

Next day he came with eggs and bread. She waited for him with a pile of stone. This blow-fly was enmeshed again. She had him trapped. A tougher cousin would have sent her packing that first day, without a second thought. There'd be no bacon twist. This cousin was too kind. He paid the price. Next day he brought my mother milk. She paid for it with flint.

I do not recall what happened then, except that those two, three bashful men with mischief on their minds soon spied my mother's industry. They were emboldened to allow her to collect their flint as well. It must have seemed – you know the wily artifice of men – that Doe's new task of piling stone would lead them closer to tasks more shared and intimate.

So now we had four sleds to load, and more to come. We were employed. Our faces were well known. The stoneys who were used to labour for themselves were quick to welcome and to use this unexpected, new resource. They saw the logic of our lives, and why we chose to live half-way between the stoneys and the stone. It made good sense that they should spend more time tapping gently at their flints, unfastening the implements that hid within, while we – for apples, eggs and bread – brought in the stone, took back the waste, maintained the hill. No one could say to us again, "That hill is ours, not yours."

25

THIS IS THE WAY MY early childhood passed.

Like all the other stoneys there we rose at dawn. It was the light that woke us. The more we were accepted, the more there was for us to do. My first job was coaxing from the embers of our fire an early flame, then warming stones for us to heat our bread. So silent was my mother at those times, that I am startled that I learned to talk. Yet talk I did, non-stop. I was a woodland bird, my father said. My mother had become as voiceless, distant as a kite. I had become a warbler in love with its own song. Here was the proof – if there was any doubt – that children are soon free of what their parents are. If I was heir to anything, it was my father's, my false father's tongue. I shared, too, his reticence with stone.

Yet on those mornings when the skies were pink and calm and the ocean wind was shy to come ashore, that hawk that father used to decorate his tales could spy me taking at a sprint the gradient between our house and the flinty hill. My mother, Doe, still half-awake on this latest day of labour, was less eager to begin. But, once at work, she was more diligent than me. She did not pause, bent double like a broken fern, in her job of loading stone on sled. She felt, at last, that she and I were safe so long as there were stoneys needing stone, so long as there were farmers, horsemen, fishers, wrights, who wanted arms and tools.

For all my sprinting and my talk I was a lazy child. It was more fun to chase the rabbits or to test how far stray seeds would fly if tossed into the wind, than work. It was more fun to make up songs, aloud, with teasing rhymes. It was more fun to mime a little constipation so that I could creep away to see what lay beyond the village and the hill.

But Doe was not amused by me. Her love – so light and pliant on the heath – was solemn on the hill. Her nightmare was that she would die and I would be alone. If she could pass to me the gift of stones, then she could die and leave me with the means to live alone. And so it was, despite the sneeze of tethered horses in the distant wood, despite the plumes of smoke which summoned from the outside world, despite the lure of father and his idle life upon the shore, I found myself enslaved.

This is how we worked. My mother used an antler pick to pierce and loosen chalk. She broke it up and pushed away the noduled roots of flint which were the tougher siblings of the chalk. She knew the trick required to spot the grain inside the stone. She knew which flints would make long knives, which were the densest, most resistant stones ideal for hammers, strikers, axe-blades, picks, which were loose enough in grain, shape and disposition to flake for arrow-heads or spears, which would splinter into harpoon barbs, which were only good for putting into walls. She sorted flints in piles and pointed to the one which I should lift and load. And then the next stone. And the next stone too. All day. That is how the job was done. We grazed and turned the earth like goats except our cud was flint not grass.

We were not good at loading all the stone on sleds. The studs and hollows would not embrace for us, or if they did, the journey down the slope towards the village would rattle loose the flint and we – in full view of every idle stoney there – would have to start again. Instead we used large baskets made from reed which we had traded in the market-place for surplus bacon earned through shifting stone. We tied the baskets on the sled. We went to every workshop in the village – including Leaf's – and came away with food or skin or fuel. The stoneys treated mother much as the merchants treated them. That is to say they treated her with all the coldness and respect with which fishermen treat fish. She was the chit and I the sprat who serviced them with stone. The passion that she roused amongst some men when we first came had cooled. She was more rounded and constrained. She was like them, a stoney night and day.

Here, perhaps, an eyebrow should be raised. Beware of what a mother's daughter says. I was a child – six years of age by now – and far too young to question or to judge what Doe had done and why. I'm speaking here with father's voice. His love for Doe had cooled as well. Or changed at least. His hopes were now regrets. They hardly spoke. My father stayed away. He could not bear the women she'd become, well fed and busy on the hill. He much preferred the ulcers and the dirt, her thinness and her poverty, her helplessness when she was living on the heath. He much preferred those dusks when she – called out by horsemen in the grass – said, "Hold the child. This won't take long."

She did not need him now. She had no need of any man. The labour which had made of her a slave had made her freer too. My father was the only one whose life was rid of stone. And so he used the phrase "flint-hearted and flint-tongued" to dismiss the woman he had courted for so long. She would not let him take revenge. She dealt with him as if he were someone she owed a debt. She hid from him. She would not meet his eyes. For her my father was the heath. She dare not think of him or it.

But we have missed my father and the heath. As this tale has journeyed on and brought us to that point where Doe, transformed and fattened, was working on the hill, we have felt the absence of the man whose rudder-tongue could steer us free from our small world. We are all tired of stone. We crave some geese or ships, some smoke or riders, some moonlit footprints shining like a pair of tumbling glow-worms in the damp. We crave again my father's single restless hand, the teasing undulations of his voice, his tales, his falsities.

And so I'll let my father's version take the oar again. He was the one who knew what happened next.

26

"IT WAS THE END OF SUMMER when she died (*my father said*). Who knows exactly when?

In those days when she lived so diligently beside the hill my life was what it always was. So there you see me once again upon the shore, running toes along the sand. What else was there to do before the night-time came? My days of 'simply filled my chest with air and took off down the coast' were gone. I was not well. I was a thwarted man. The song I sang was this: How sad is he who has no wife. His seed is trapped. It turns to poison in his loins. His blood runs hot and burns. It dries his body and he leads a pale and angry life.

Move on, I'd tell myself. Forget this Doe. She's lost – though quite how lost I did not guess. I was throbbing for her still. In the bony swelling of my severed arm. And elsewhere too – though I had a ready palliative for that. The cure for my arm was death. And until then, it seemed, I had to live with pain. The flint-cut bone, its covering of skin so tucked and tightly drawn, was now, as I grew older, softening and turning bad. The stump was red except where blisters formed or punctured so that pus could drain and dry. See here. My arm. This is no tale. If I wanted to invent misfortune for myself I'd not invent this arm or what occurred to Doe. I'd suffer the bad luck that mends. I'd not be me.

Watch out, you say. We know his tricks. He's milking us like cows. He thinks we'll sympathize with all his sins because his arm is bad. You're right, you're right. But I'm only telling what occurred, and my story takes its shape from what has happened to my arm. With two arms I'd be knapping and too dull and chalky to tell tales. With two arms I'd not have taken off along the coast, or killed the goose, or brought the woman and her girl back home. An arrow ruled my world; it made me what I am.

What kind of man is that? I must presume I am the vengeful sort. I've said before that malice and my elbow stump are twins. When Doe made clear that she rejected me I did not wish her well. I wanted her to see that she would suffer on her own, that I was the only straw for her to catch. I offered her gifts of food. But she was in no mood for me. She feared my tongue. She feared, I think, that I might talk about the horsemen on the heath and what she did for them and what they paid.

She clearly did not fear the tongues of those few men who courted her. She was the sweetest lamb with them. I'd watched her from afar. I'd seen the way she'd block their paths and rouse them with her smiles. I'd followed her and cousin to the hill and watched her test her charms on him. A waste of time. That blushing cousin was no use. His blood sped to his face – and nowhere else. And yet. Somehow. She'd trapped him. And herself. He'd ended up the sheepish devotee of Doe. She'd ended up a devotee of stone.

At times I wished I had less time. The hours that I passed, alone, were hours free to concentrate on pain. I saw the strength the stoneys had in focusing all day on flint. Each mallet blow, each flake, each bellow breath, each sticky cough which tried and failed to lift the chalk dust from their lungs, would cut their worries short. They did not seem to mope. Was I the only one to see that, all around, the world was tumbling, spinning, wild? The bats were flying in the sun, the butterflies at night. You only had to briefly lift your head above your parapet of stones to see that where the village ended mayhem ruled and danced.

I expect you smile and brighten in expectation of some fantasy of mine. You're weary of those tales in which the ship lands on the beach and unloads women, perfume, plagues, or sailors hunting for the sun. You've heard each variation of the way my arm was lost; the women and the beasts, the drunk and hungry traveller who mistook it for a chicken, the cruel and giant gull. You're tired of the talking goose, the magic dog, the travelling stench, the boy who had the gift of flames. You're ready for some freshly fashioned tale. The thought of mayhem dancing gives you hope. Instead, all hope ends here.

Again it starts with what I took to be a ship. One night the wind was coming off the land and sweeping out to sea. For once the rooks were flying over water and the waves, at dusk, were tossing back their heads and hair and fleeing from the beach. The sea, so used to going with the wind, had reared in anger at the way its mate had turned. It was in turmoil, like a grey and boiling pot of gruel. The wind, instead of calling 'Home, go home' was singing 'Back, keep back'. The land, so tired of all the pounding it endured, was turning on the sea.

Of course, the stoneys went inside and packed the un-protected landside of their homes with wads of moss or peat to keep away the draughts. I walked up to the avalanche of

stones and wood that Doe had built herself. I thought the
wind would turn her home into a fall of rocks and take her
and her daughter, too, in a tumbling tour of village, beach
and sea. I stood outside and called, 'Doe, Doe, Sweet Doe.
It's me.' I dare not call too loud despite the wind. My errand
was too shy.

At last, when she had offered no reply, I pushed aside
the flapping gate-screen to their home. I sensed the bodies
lying there. Doe's tense and wakeful breaths. The quaver of
the sleeping girl. The wrestling of the wind and walls.

'It's me,' I said again, though, in that light, me might
have been one of a dozen men.

'What is it, then?' she asked.

'Are you all right?'

'Of course.'

'It's windy out.'

'We're used to wind.'

I went outside and propped my back against the dry,
land wind. I heard but could not see the sea. Yet there were
yellow lights. It seemed as if there were three stars which had
taken refuge in the shallow water just offshore. They seemed
to bob and shift. These were the kind of lights to make a story
bob and shift as well. They were the lights of ghosts or
lightning fish or baby stars which hatched from surf; they
were the early lights of windswept dawn or the spitting
embers of the dusk, if that is what I chose.

But what I choose now is to tell the truth. Those lights
– turned frantic in the bay – were sailors bringing in their boat
and doing what they could with burning brands to find a
passage free of rocks. Their ship was stray, exhausted, blown
off-course by storms. You hold your breath to hear the tale of

how I met the sailors on the beach. You've heard that one before, though not in wind and not at night. But here my tale is done. They sheltered from the wind. And in the morning they had gone. I did not fill my lungs with air and take off down the coast. Which coast? Which way?

A few days later, with the wind and sea now reconciled, I saw three sails far out. And, in the afternoon, two more. All of them were heading for the coast beyond the place where Doe had had her hut. I was reminded of those days when the geese came in, first singly, then in skeins. These ships were just as buoyant, and as stately, as the birds. Why was there mayhem in my mind?

Here is the paradox of ships. Our hearts should lift at sails, because they show that every tumult of the seas is weaker than the will of sailors. A ship is order, symmetry. Its line is straight, its purpose clear; it has no moods. Yet my heart sank when I saw ships in such numbers, in such rhythmic unison, heading for the shore. It felt as if an older symmetry had been betrayed, the symmetry of tides and waves, and of an horizon shimmering and dimpled for the passage of the sun, not sails. Those ships caused me alarm. They made me fear that wads of moss were not enough to keep the world at bay.

What next? The rooks again. They rose like gnats above the waving masts of trees in the forests beyond the hill. Something on the ground had frightened them, was frightening them each day. And then the fires, though distant, seemed to burn too thickly. The smoke was heavy, grey, long-lived. The sea-borne chaos had come ashore and was setting villages alight. What other meanings could there be to the sequence of the ships, the rooks, the fires?

What would you have done if you were me? Run up and tell the stoneys, Look, the smoke is thick, the rooks are high, they're not there now but there were ships upon the sea, your world is coming to an end? Would that have caused alarm? It would have caused, instead, delight. They would have sent for me at night and asked me to repeat it all while they relaxed and ate. And if I made them step outside and look beyond the hill at smoke and rooks? What then? They'd only marvel at the power of my tongue. The ritual of our trade was this – I did not tell the truth. They looked to me for comfort not for gloom.

Of course, a man must eat and food for me was earned by talk. I did invent for them another breed of tales in which a fleet of ships with crews, half-rook, half-man, had come to land. They lived on fire. Flames were their meat. Their drink was smoke. Or else (for children) a tribe of giants had come ashore and in their haste to devastate the land had knocked a rook's egg from its nest. The story was the rook's revenge. The moral was the power of the weak. Or else the men that came ashore were armed with weapons that were gleaming in the oddest way. The stones that made them were as light as leaves; their arrows sped like swallows. Compared, our arrows were like pigeons, plump and clumsy in the air.

This last was not a favourite tale. The stoneys and the merchants were aware that trade in flint was bad. The market-place was not the bustle it had been. There were fewer horse-men passing through with enticing goods to trade for arms. Although the farmers still arrived to barter what they grew for what we made, there were old trading friends who seemed to disappear.

Who dared discuss this, openly, aloud? Not anyone I

knew. They only whispered that perhaps there was a plague, a war, some floods, which kept the trade away. They did not doubt that life – despite its passing oddities – would go their way quite soon. This was the lesson they had learned whenever trade had slackened in the past: the outside world was never free from stone. There was no sickling of the corn, no scraping hides, no fishing, hunting, wars, no cutting flesh, no knives, no fires, except for stone and stoneys. Without the stoneys men would have to fight with sticks. And what would women use to cut the cord when children came? Their teeth? What next? Were people just as mean as wolves?

And so the merchants waited, unconcerned. They had stocks. They did not barter with the stoneys for more tools. They'd wait – and, maybe, falling trade would prove to their advantage in a while. They'd pay the stoneys less for flints while demand was low. And when demand increased again? Only a fool expects largesse in trade.

What of the stoneys? It was clear that for a while their flints could not be sold in quite the numbers that they'd hoped. They used the time they saved on making tools by mending walls or building beds or finishing those thousand tasks that had built up, like dust, around the house. If anything, a mite unnerved, they worked a little harder than before. They were like bats. They had to flap and fly. If they put down upon the ground for rest, they knew they'd never fly again.

So, to the point. What do I know of Doe? One thing's for sure, her sled was not at work. The stoneys were not making tools. There was no merchant with the will to say More Stone and for his will to set the villagers to work and for the villagers to dispatch Doe for sleds of flint. Where there's no work then people starve. Doe and her daughter were the first to learn. They searched for rabbits, berries, nuts. But there were none. The villagers lived where they lived because the hill was full of stone, not because the soil was rich or the undergrowth a busy universe of untrapped, unpicked food.

I could not invent for you a better recipe for mischief – the world haywire with ships and fires; the woman, hungry, desperate; the men, denied their stone, with time and minor tasks upon their hands. It does not take a minstrel to make that story rhyme. It only needed Doe to put her hand upon the arm of some shy stoney passing by, or for some man, emboldened by the bony weakness of poor Doe, to touch her buttocks or her waist, for what I'd witnessed on the heath to happen in our village, too. I've said before, I spied on her. Why not? I only dreamed that I might save her or the girl from falling rocks, or wind, or wolves. So watching her was just my way of mounting guard. Yet it was not rocks or wind or wolves that made me want to run clear from my hiding place and save her from herself. It was my eldest cousin, the slow and cheerful one. She took him to the bracken and returned with apples and with cheese. He walked off by himself, more stooped and thoughtful than he had been when Doe had met him on the path.

I watched her other times with other men. She did not starve. And once there was a bonus. She found mushrooms near the spot where she and one young man had lain. She shared them with the girl that night, while I awaited dawn, as cold, unloved and venomous as viper's dew.

I was a man made hollow. I cannot tell if it was rage or love or lunacy that sent me running at first light through the village to the shore and then along the coast in search of samphire for my Doe. We'd let the flesh embrace; we'd watch the stems whine and bubble in the fire like spit in love. My stem, her flesh, our love. That was my thought as, arm in pain, I ran and ran along the path that took me to the heath.

You know the route. I'll not detail the landmarks that are old friends to us. The samphire was moist and smooth, and flourishing, unpicked, where once the geese had died. There were no signs of huts upon the heath. There were no rooks or ships or fires. There was just the samphire and the juicy rocks and wind. I picked her fill. Me filling her was all I had in mind. I marvelled at my speed and skill, and at the luck which brought me through the bracken, over rocks, without a sprain or scratch.

I reached the village at the end of evening with a little owl-light, dim and looming on the land. I went straight to her home. I called out, 'Rabbit, Rabbit, Doe,' and held the samphire high above my head – a challenge – in my one and only hand. This was no gift. I'd come to pay. But she had gone. Her daughter ran to me as if I were the only one to trust. She hung on to my waist. Her tale was this – that Doe had gone off with a man at noon. She still had not returned."

27

"WHAT COULD I DO AT night? Not much, except to stay awake and sketch out in my mind the likely fates of Doe. The girl was still too young to fear much more than being by herself at night. Now I was there she stretched out on her back and slept. I did not try to sleep. I sat up like a widow on a grave. If Doe came back, I would not wish to be a snuffling body in her bed.

Perhaps, I thought, she's found some coterie of men who want her for the night. They've paid her extra nuts or eggs to sleep with them till dawn. I ought to light a brand and walk about the village, calling out, 'Own up! Who's tupping Doe? Which men are blunting blades with her?'

Instead I dwelled on what might seem a less than likely reason for her absence in the night. She'd taken off, like me, and, desperate with loathing for her life, had run towards the heath. Perhaps she'd blundered past me as I returned. What I had taken as a rabbit, sent frantic in the undergrowth by me, had been a Rabbit of a larger kind. If we had met, both breathless on the cliff-top path, among the winkle-berries and the ferns, and our collision had not spun us crashing to the beach, then what certain congress there'd have been. Imagine how the village kept us both apart. Imagine how the cliff, the wind, the sea, the samphire on my arm, would bring us close again. At last, the prospect sent me off to sleep.

Doe did not return that night. I asked the villagers who passed if they had seen her. They had not. I spoke in whispers to those men I knew had been with her. They shook their heads. They had no time to talk. No, they'd never been such friends with Doe, they said. It was their view that my tongue was running loose again. And they'd see to it that if I didn't strap it down I'd find myself in trouble, and quite soon.

It seemed that no one knew of Doe. They had more pressing problems of their own. While I'd been picking samphire on the heath a troop of horsemen had ridden through the village at great speed. Their horses had knocked merchants down, and injured some. And frightened all. They had not stopped to trade. The villagers were now subdued and inward, like bleatless sheep who've smelt the scent of circling wolves and turned for comfort to an open patch of grass.

Was I the only one that moved at speed? I ran towards the hill, exactly in the way that I had run that morning long ago when all the village boys and girls had helped open up the new flint shaft, that morning when I slipped away to dine on rabbit with outsiders in the distant wood. I passed Doe's house of stones where her daughter – at my bidding – sat and waited at the door. I passed between the sentries made of rock. And when I reached the summit of the hill I stood upon the fattest, tallest flint. I was the one-armed sentinel of all the land and sea below. I looked for rooks and ships and smoke. There were no ships. The only rooks were labouring the air about their roosts with calm and even wings. What smoke there was was ours. It came from stoney fires.

I knew no sight more sad than that – the sight of that small, kempt place, its walls as ordered and as uniform as ribs laid bare, its life as timorous, fettered and discreet as that enjoyed by barnacles on stone. And all around and all beyond, in blues and greys and greens, and fading far away into the whites of distance and of sky, was all the outside world. It seemed as if the outside world was like a mist and the mist was closing in. And all our world was shrinking, breath by breath. Someone, something, was hovering between our village and the sun.

They say in villages more fanciful than ours that when you die you hover like a hawk above your home. Your life assembles there. Your mother and your father who died so long ago are sitting side by side. You see yourself as baby, child and man. You shed no tears. You – like a hawk – spread out your wings and fly between your lifetime and the sun. The beating shadow that you cast falls like a blessing and farewell on to yourself as baby, child and man. 'Beware the shadow of a hawk,' they say. 'It buries men.'

It was a hawk that led me to poor Doe. The shadow that I'd felt at first was cloud. It touched me with its drops of rain. But the dimming, stubborn shadow that held my eye was hawk. It hovered over bracken on the exposed brow between Leaf's home and sea. The bracken looked as if it had been hit by wind. It was flattened in a swathe. So that was where the horsemen had galloped through in so much haste and disarray. I wondered if the hawk was seeking beetles in the horses' dung. I watched it drop and walk, as cocky as a magpie, in the swathe. And then I saw what seemed like someone dozing in the bracken a little distance from the horses' path. The shadow of the hawk – I swear – passed over it and did not stop until it was a speck above the sea.

You think I'm weaving words? Then run with me down to the bracken path. Your heart is stone if you are not afraid.

That 'someone dozing' must be Doe. That body must be dead. I found her flat upon her back. Her head was on its side. The gulls had had her eyes. One leg was twisted, one arm was turned. Her hands were weighing down her smock. Her fingers were as straight and cold and blue as razor shells. At her side a dozen scallops lay, sticky with her blood. I could not see the wound until I knelt to straighten out her arm and leg. And then I saw the wound deep in the shallow waist-dell of her back. I saw the arrow, too. And pulled it out. And wiped it clean. And wondered at its weight and shape and shine."

28

"THIS IS THE STORY OF Doe's death.

A man had come for her at noon. We do not know his name – but let it be my cousin. He will do. He was his usual timid self. He gave Doe apples and some bread.

'Why can't we do it here?' he asked. 'The girl can play outside.'

But Doe said no. 'This place is ours. Not yours.'

They went outside and when she saw the way he looked along the path towards the village to check that no one came, her indifference for him was transformed. Her mood was fashioned out of equal helpings of levity and spite. Why should he feel such shame at passing time with her? She had the apples and the bread. What else was there to lose?

My cousin took Doe by the wrist and pulled her to the beaten bracken where normally she lay down with her men. There was a freckled patch of flattened bracken pits as evidence of trade.

'Not there,' she said. 'My daughter is too close.'

She pulled my cousin back onto the path.

'Come on,' she said, in a voice more intimate and teasing than she had used before. 'I know a private place.'

She took him by the hand and walked with him downhill towards the village. His passion for her soon became embarrassment. He took his hand away from hers. He tried to make it seem that their descent into the village was a chance encounter, nothing more. He grew alarmed when he heard voices or the rasp of bellows or the click of stone. He fell behind – so now she walked ahead as if she were the greater of the two. And he hung back, half-mesmerized by Doe and how she walked and the allure of when she'd said, 'I know a private place,' and half-wishing that he'd never left the workshop with the excuse that he was looking for some wood for hafts.

'Come on,' she called, as they approached the market-green where, idle from the dearth of trade, the merchants were like owls, fat-faced, big-eyed and missing nothing. They saw the woman. It was true what they had heard. She was as wild and skinny as a stoat. Yet, like a stoat, she was a pleasing sight. I wonder what she'd do for, say, a bone of perfume, one merchant wondered in a whisper meant for everyone to hear. And then they saw my sheepish cousin in her wake. He had no choice. He became as solemn as a stone. He asked some merchants if they had good wood for hafts. They saw his hands were empty and they asked what goods he had to trade. They said that wood was not so cheap that it could be purchased with fistfuls of air. My bashful cousin blushed. No one there was fooled. His contract with my mother was as visible as if the two were sharing just one smock. Besides, the woman was beckoning and holding out her hand and calling, 'Come on, come on, you were so hurried just a while ago.'

'Clear off,' my cousin said, to laughter all around.

'And what about the apples and the bread you paid?'

'There were no apples and no bread,' my cousin told the merchants who sat there.

'Then we are quits,' my mother said. 'No pay, no play.'

All eyes – with every eyebrow raised – were now upon my cousin. They understood the tangle he was in. They saw the woman loop and tie the knots that bound him.

At last he said, 'Her head's a mushroom. She's quite mad.' And then: 'My family has been kind to her. We let her load the sled and bring us flint. We give her bread and apples for her child. For all that she's a numskull and a clod we treat her better than a sister. . . .'

That one word 'sister' made the merchants honk. They were as merry as a swarm of grigs. The lack of clients and of trade had made them indiscreet and playful. For them my cousin, self-impaled and writhing like a half-hooked eel, was an entertainment and an excuse for jollity and smut. So when he seized the nearest object to his hand – a leather purse – and threw it after Doe, the merchants doubled up with guffaws and with stitch. And when the purse – so inexpertly thrown – merely looped and curled into the wind and fell a child's length from my cousin's feet, some men there wondered if their sides would hold and whether this was laughter or a fit.

For once, my Doe felt warm and welcome with these men. Her laughter was as loud as theirs. Her face was flushed and happy. They called out to her, 'Good for you' and 'Well said, sister!'

Their approbation was a sign for her to leave. She left my cousin there and, rather than retrace her steps and unravel the good humour she had woven for herself and them, she continued to that private place, the long grass on the headland beyond Leaf's home.

You've heard before how, from above, the beach viewed

from the cliff-top is a world that's upside down. Its gulls have backs. You're looking down on wind. So Doe looked down on wind, and on the mirror pools which were as blue or cloudy as the passing sky. The tide was pulling back. Each wave was more tremulous and more distant than the one which went before. The sand was beating back the sea.

You can imagine what it was that summoned Doe down from her private place. The sea-shore is a lure for those with time upon their hands. Who can resist the bribe and charm of shells or sand or pebble-stones? Only stoneys, it would seem, too occupied with work and trade to savour all the smells and flavours of the beach.

And so my story places her right at the water's edge. The sun was on her back, the wind was in her face. Her feet were bare. She dug her toes into the sand. And then she must have felt the shiver of a living thing beneath her feet. She curled her toes and pulled it out. It was a scallop, taking refuge from the light. She tried again with both feet now. She must have looked as if she wished to fight the wind by gripping to the shore with toes. Quite soon she found that if she stood exactly where the tide gave way to sand, the scallops, slamming shut their wings, threw out a jet of water which marked exactly where they hid. She collected for herself a dozen scallops, as many shells as she could hold and still climb up the rocks to reach the village path. She wondered at the comments she would get when she marched through the market-place enriched by scallops and by sea.

She did not reach the market-place, despite the orders of the wind which spat and whispered at her back, 'Go home. Go home.' She heard the thunder of the horses before she reached Leaf's house. She knew enough of horsemen to retreat. She stepped into the bracken and sat down. She placed her scallops on the ground. She heard the cries and curses of the merchants as the troop of horsemen hurtled through, knocking men and merchandise aside. She heard the snapping heather as the horsemen passed Leaf's house and turned towards the coast. She felt as fragile as a plover's egg, abandoned on the ground. She saw herself turned into porridge by a hundred hooves. She stood up in the bracken and waved her arms to warn the horsemen she was there. One rider, alarmed perhaps by what he took to be a sudden threat, found time to pause and draw an arrow in his bow. He welcomed the excuse to let it loose, this sharp and shiny leaf, this bronze. She saw him and she turned her back to flee. His arrow was more swift than her. It caught her and she fell.

Or else? Or else the scallops were not hers but found by someone else. A man. My cousin, let us say. Who can tell what brought him to the beach, the morning of the day she died? Of all my cousins he was the truant one. He was the one most ill at ease with brothers and with work. Perhaps that now there was less work to do and little food from trade, he thought he'd try his luck at my one skill – not telling tales but hunting with my toes. No doubt – a stoney to his heart – he will have felt forlorn upon the beach, exposed, and bored, and cold. It would have seemed to him a damp and dirty task to unearth scallops and, once his sling was full, we can imagine how he fled the sea and sand for the order of the village.

His first thought was to take the scallops home, but they would spread too thinly if he shared. If he could have found an unattended fire he would have baked them for himself.

Such scallops, after all, would make a change from bread and
apples and dry meat. And then his second thought was this:
he'd take the scallops to the woman on the hill. For once she
would not make a fool of him. For scallops she would do what
she was told.

He found the woman and her girl half-asleep and sheltered in the clumsy cave of stones and wood that they called
home. She seemed more flimsy than she'd been when she'd
survived by sledding stone. She told the girl to wait and
pointed to the bracken a few paces downwind from the
path.

'Let's go there,' she said and held her hand out for the
sling of shells which he had promised her.

'Afterwards,' he said. He felt triumphant and in charge.
He knew how hungry she must be. Her eagerness for him
and them would fade as soon as his fresh and salty bribe
change hands. He gripped the sling and pulled Doe to the
ground.

That would have been the end of that. My cousin would
not be the patient, careful sort. His passion was short-lived.
Except the girl was calling, 'Doe' and whimpering.

'Stay there. I won't be long,' her mother called.

'Can I go, too?'

My cousin found it hard to concentrate when the woman
he had bought was shouting conversations in the wind. He
pulled my mother to her feet. 'Come on,' he said. 'I know a
private place.'

She went with him because she had the scallops on her
mind. He said, 'I'll walk ahead. You follow me.'

He led her through the village and across the market-
green. The stoneys and the merchants were too preoccupied

with worries of their own to pay attention to my cousin or to Doe. All kinds of people passed by them. Why should they notice who went where with whom? You can't sell gossip – gossip's free.

When they had passed the moss-packed walls of Leaf's stone house my cousin paused for Doe to take his hand. It would have seemed a touching sight for simpletons, the awkward, blushing man, the meagre Doe, the fragrance of the bracken and romance. The stoneys seldom passed by here. They were not fond of cliffs or sea. And so my cousin felt emboldened by their privacy. He did not understand what she was trading for his shells. He thought he'd purchased her affection with his trophies from the beach. He thought each scallop would secure a kiss from Doe. He made a nuisance of himself.

'Come on,' she said. 'Let's not waste time. You've brought me all this way and I've a daughter waiting for me and for food.'

Doe led the way into the bracken and – that painful, reminiscent lifting of her smock – she stood ready to receive my cousin and his shells. She might have been upon the heath once more. Her thighs were punctured water bags. Her breasts were flat. Her face was reddening with hidden sores. Her eyes were beaten and appalled at the prospect of her task which made of her both the trader and the labourer. She was the merchandise as well. My cousin's role was more clear. His clothes were off and he was holding Doe as if she were as light and worthless as a shock of reeds.

They should have hidden when they heard the horse-men come, but Doe could not distinguish cry from cry or heart beats from hooves. It was too late to hide once the troop of riders had reached the clifftop path beyond Leaf's walls and turned their horses. They had been seen, two nearly naked bodies, standing waist-high in bracken. Who knows what mischief made one rider pause and loose one arrow at my cousin and at Doe? It was the kind of mischief that makes men kick down toadstools or snub a passing beetle with their thumb. Those chance-encountered things – untouched – seem far too innocent, insubstantial, perfect, to pass and leave unscathed. It must have seemed too good a chance to miss – the prospect of dividing those two lovers by the sea.

The arrow's flight was even and too swift for Doe to move or sink. She simply joined my cousin in his panic as he twisted her around to shield his naked flesh with hers. The bronze and shiny leaf was like a yellow-throated diver when it hit her skin, the point its beak, her flesh the sea, its fish the kidney in the woman's back. Its impact was as neat and light as those which open up a flint to show the blade within.

The rider did not wait to see what damage he had done. His horse was separated from the rest and he must give pursuit. Nor did my cousin wait to see. He dropped the scallops, turned and ran. For all he knew the horseman would return to put an end to him. You cannot blame him for his flight. But what he should have done was this. He should have run straight to the market-green and told his neighbours there about the woman and her wound. They could have armed themselves with sticks and come to take her home. But he said nothing. He just ran, by routes which took him to his house avoiding stoneys and the market-green. He hoped her wound was only slight, that he would spot her, once again, outside her hillside home. What was the point, he asked himself, of letting all the world into the secret of his trade with Doe when she was only scratched or bruised or shocked? When it was dark he'd climb up to her house to check that she was well.

She fell onto the bracken with a pain which came in waves like childbirth. She fell onto the arrow and snapped the shaft and drove the head more deeply in. She was unconscious fairly soon, with shock, fatigue and pain. What were her dreams? We'll never know. Her face was pale. The earth was damp and dark with blood.

Or else she did not die just then. Or else she did not die like that. The gossip on the green was this, that I'd been spotted on that day. I'd been along the cliffs and come back to the village with my bag full-gutted with the free food of the coast. Who knows what else I hid inside my bag? An arrow-head perhaps?

Anyone that saw me then, they said, would wonder at the luck and skill which brought the one-armed man through thickets, over rocks, without a wound or fall. I had a purpose. What it was they could not guess. But there was a saying, the agile and the speedy ram is the one with sheep in view. My sheep was Doe. How well they could remember that first night when I had brought the woman and her girl to the village. The refugees had slept, exhausted by the walk, while I had told my cousins and their friends the story of Doe's life. They'd fled before the tale was done, both bored and irritated by the passion and the anger in my voice. My ailment was too clear. I was besotted with the skinny woman from the heath. It did not take a sage to see that love like mine – belittled, spurned – would turn to poison once the object of that love became the willing consort of all men but me. The gossip made a killer out of me. It seems the stoneys hadn't got enough to do – already they were telling stories of their own.

So let me pick their story up. They've left it as a rough and ready core. The craftsman in me wants to strike it softly here and there, to give it shape and symmetry, to hone and burnish it. Imagine, then, that I've been telling lies. I found fresh samphire for Doe's gift not on the heath but much nearer to the village. It flourished on a stream bank where a shallow valley joined the coast. It was where I'd lit the fire with hair. I picked the samphire and found, too, a colony of scallops in the tidal sand. My bag was full. I had no other tasks. Besides, the fresh hoof-marks in the mud and sand were warnings that there were horsemen close. There were the embers of a second fire, some flattened grass, some rabbit bones, a broken arrow-shaft with the smoothest, lightest head which was not stone. That, too, I put inside my bag. I was unnerved by what I found. I hurried home. And so I returned to the village in the early afternoon and not at night as I have said.

Remember what my plan had been? I'd take the scallops and the samphire to Doe's house. I was as hollow and as brittle as a blown egg with jealousy. I'd stand outside and call, 'Doe, Doe, sweet Doe.' And when she came? I'd pay. I'd fall down on my knees. I'd throw her samphire as a gift. I'd be as giddy as a goat. I could invent a thousand reconcilations.

Instead, I heard the sound of calling in the bracken which stood between the sea and Leaf.

'Come on,' she said. 'Let's not waste time.' It was Doe's voice. And the man that she addressed was my sheepish cousin. He seemed less sheepish for a while. He was shedding clothes as if they were alive and venomous. The Doe I saw was just the same as that first sight upon the heath when she had offered shelter from the rain and we had dined on slott. That was the day I pulled that first and modest screen of grass across my tale. If I'd been wise I would have let the bracken and the grass provide another screen. I should have shut my eyes and ears or run down to the shore. But jealousy is like a moth – it seeks the brightest flame.

I was close enough to see her buttocks and her back, to watch her smock rise up, to witness cousin – erect and tremulous – enclose her in his arms. What might I have done had not the troop of horsemen passed close by? Thrown scallop shells, perhaps? Or crept away? Or strode into the clearing they had made and, with my one arm round Doe's waist, have said, 'This woman's mine, not yours. I found her on the heath. I brought her here. Who said that you could take my Doe?' Then I might have struck my cousin on his mouth like some possessive stoney beaten to a flint. And he – the soft and cheerful sort – would have simply turned and fled.

Instead I remained hidden while the horsemen galloped past. They were in too much haste and fear to even notice those two people, those two nearly naked bodies standing waist high in the bracken. We could hear cries from the market-green. My cousin was alarmed. He wondered what had happened to his family, his home. He ran – his clothes half on and off – into the swathe of broken stems where the riders had just passed. He called to Doe that she should dress and hurry, too. Who knows what dangers there might be with horsemen so close by?

There was no time for her to leave. In moments I was at her side and throwing samphire in her face and pelting her with shells. The riders had invaded me. Their flight, their speed, their carelessness. What must it be to simply fly on hooves like that, to be the two-armed horseman in the wind? That demon part of me which lived in caves was now set loose. It was as weathered as a piece of bark. It had a horseman's squint. You'd take its face to be a leather purse with teeth. It knew no bounds. The woman's dignity beneath its blows, her independence as she fell, only increased its rage. She was a goose. She was a mortar full of corn. She was no more than stone. And yet she spoke. She said, 'What kind of friend are you? You don't touch me.'

She would have crawled away, just bruised, if that odd, smooth arrow-head had not fallen from my bag. I picked it up and – so the gossip goes – I plunged it in her back."

29

ENOUGH. MY FATHER'S STORIES ARE a mask. I owe it to my mother and to him to tell you only what is known and not what he would wish us to believe. Doe had bled to death for sure and father had, indeed, found her beneath the shadow of the hawk. He had wiped clean the arrow-head, and placed his ear against my mother's chest. She was entirely cold and still. In that my father told the truth. She was no more than stone.

It was not easy for a one-armed man whose stump was swollen and in pain, whose eyes were full, to lift my mother from the ground and balance her across his back. And then to stoop and to pick up the arrow-head. And then to walk with them through bracken to the springy path which joined the village and the shore. For once he did not feel the wind and spray upon his back. My mother was his shield.

The stoneys and the merchants were quite used to seeing father on that path. It was the path which led him to the outside world and on which he would return weighed down and weary with new tales. The magic ship had come that way. The talking goose. The boy who had the gift of flames. It would not seem so strange to see my father stooped and slow returning to them by that route. What he carried on his back, that shining something in his hand, they took to be some teasing evidence with which he'd complicate his lies.

In fact he did not say a word. He had no breath. He put the body on the grass and, holding mother by an ankle, sat down at her feet. He placed the arrow-head on her chest.

It was some time before the first brave men found time and inclination to take a closer look. My father's world and Doe's was hardly theirs. They felt no duty to the corpse. Unlike the people from beyond the wood they did not fear the dead. They saw no need to truss up the bodies of the slain or to placate them with provisions for the grave. For them the dead were powerless. They could not punish those who lived. They had no weapons of revenge. They had not been liberated from this world to carry out some mischievous design. There were no ghosts. But still, a woman dead and murdered – at a guess – by those same men who had swept through the market-place and knocked the merchants down, was cause for some alarm. There'd be no recompense, for sure. Those horsemen did not seem the sort who'd pay their debts or recognize the rules of trade. They were the sort to fear.

"What happened here?" My father wet his lips to make reply. But he had no chance to speak. A stoney had sunk down onto his knees and, leaning over Doe, was staring at the weapon on her chest.

"What's this?" he said. He hesitated for a moment as if to seek some reason why he could not take the object off the corpse. And then he reached and lifted it. "So light," he said. "So smooth."

My father's neighbours turned their backs on Doe. They

passed the arrow-head from hand to hand and shook their heads. They did not know this stone – if stone it was. There were no flattened planes or impact dents where the hammer stone had struck. There were no fractures at the arrow's stem, or facets where the arrow had been flaked. The blade was flat and thinner than a cuttle shell. It was hard and sharp. Its surface was the colour of winter oak-leaves and as smooth and cold to touch as bacon skin. Then one man noticed what the rest had missed. He pulled the broken wooden shaft from the arrow-head. He pushed his little finger in the hole it left and held it up for all his friends to see. At first they were confused. And then they knew that flint was second-best. This stem was something flint could never be, as hollow as an acorn cup and twenty times as deep.

They turned upon my father now. What kind of tale was this? Invention was my father's craft. They thought the arrow-head was father's trick. "Come on," they said. "Let's hear."

I do not know which of the many tales he told or who he blamed or how my mother died. If he'd invented naked warriors who'd slid down lightning from the sky, or animals, half-horse half-wolf, who'd sworn vengeance on the world, the stoneys would have taken it. Their sense of what was true or not was punctured by the arrow-head. A world that could produce a weapon as perfect and as beautiful as that could produce a thousand wonders of my father's sort. In fact my father did not try to concoct a story to explain the arrow-head. He turned it in his hand and shrugged and claimed he was as ignorant as them. But we know father and we tense when we hear him using phrases of that kind. "I'm just as ignorant as you," he said, "of where this arrow has come from, or where the stone, or where the people with such craft. Not here. Not us, for sure." And then the one-armed village story-teller voiced the one thought that lay siege to everybody's mind. He said, "So now we know why trade in flint is bad."

30

THERE WAS NO POINT IN asking father to say more. That winter was the worst he'd known. It froze what bones he had. He was a silent man. He feared the questions, Where is my mother? What's become of Doe?

Together we found food enough for two. We lived, but thinly. I'd learnt and father guessed or knew which plants were good, what seaweed could be warmed and chewed, how grubs took refuge under bark, where toadstools could be found, where nuts. Each morning we went gathering ebb meat on the shore, dead fish or crabs. We were competing with the seagulls and the tide. And on those days when there was nothing else my father showed me how to pull the frosted roots of famine grass. The secret was to twist and tug. The roots were sweet to taste but bitter in the gut.

You need not fear for us. We'd come through worse, and still had tales to tell. You might, instead, direct your sympathy downhill. The stoneys were a dying breed. This was the age of smiths. There was no trade for us at all. Who'd want to hoe their soil with stone when stone might splinter on the frost? Who'd go for flint when tools in flint would flake with too much use? Now flint was only good for walls and tombs. For implements and arms, the world demanded bronze.

The gift of bronze, they said, had come by ships. My father nodded; he had seen the fleet. The sailors and the merchants and the smiths had put ashore. They'd found where metals could be mined. They settled there. The merchants who passed through – and, seeing our dilemma, did not stop for trade – would, pestered by the knappers, tease us all with displays of their bronze, their repertoire of shapes and decorations, their startling merchandise.

Here were heads for hoes and mallets, scythes, with moulded holes and knobs to hold the wooden shaft. Here were blades with ribs, with spines, with knuckles where the swordsman put his thumb. And here were knives that matched the shape of chestnut leaves, the curve of carps' tongues, the coolness of icicles. The merchants showed us axes that had wings, and helmets horned like rams, and beaten shields as round and gleaming as the sun, and knives with pommels engraved with claws or snakes or eyes. In rabbit-skins were wrapped the finest works of bronze: necklaces and rings, pins and brooches, plates and harness bells.

The stoneys looked on in dismay. Their flint could not complete. It was too innocent and dull. They listened without comprehension while the passing traders told of how the bronze was mined and mixed and made. It took, they said, two hands of copper to each thumb of tin. And then you'd need some charcoal and a pit and some bellows with a mouth of clay. A fire was lit inside the pit. And when it cooled a metal plug was formed. That was the easy part. A child could tackle that. The craft was in the moulding and the beating of the bronze, the removal of the flashes and the casting jets, the details of design.

There was a question that they asked amongst themselves. The question was, Who found this out and why? Who first thought to mine for copper, tin, to measure it in hands and thumbs, to charge it in a pit with charcoal, to pour it in a mould? With what in mind? And why? It was quite clear how the first knappers got to work. You only need to throw a stone to see it break and view the sinews and the flesh within. An idle child with nothing else to do would soon find out that flint was sharp and hard. But bronze? It made no sense.

My father had some stories which would explain the mysteries of bronze. But the stoneys did not wish to hear. They knew their village was exposed. They were obsessed by that. The scripture – that they could not be touched because they had the gift of stones – had been proved false. They felt like carcasses while all around were gulls and rooks and wolves.

Have pity, then, on gulls and rooks and wolves. They'd not dine well. Our neighbours were as thin as Doe. Their carcasses were only skin and bone. The sockets of their eyes were large and rimmed from sleeplessness. Their skin was rough and dry, their noses damp. They lived on what was left from better days. They were too timorous to forage on the hillside or the shore. They couldn't tell good food from weed. They'd drink salt water from the sea. They'd feed themselves with sand.

Of course, our merchants remained fat. They had reserves of food. They'd set aside some grain and meat to trade with in the early spring. So now they traded with themselves. A merchant who had dried fruit could make a friend of one with hams. But merchants are not merchants without fresh merchandise. It was not very long before some traders packed and left. There was no profit left in flint and they would have to start anew, elsewhere, before their riches were used up. They bartered for some horses and some sleds and, while we gathered round to watch, they packed all their possessions and set off towards the place where bronze was made. Their future was with bronze, they said. They only hoped that if the outside world was wild with horsemen and with war, their tongues and merchandise could purchase passage to a market which was as safe – and profitable – as ours had been. We did not wish them luck – or well. Not even when the final trader left. We did not doubt that they'd be wealthy once again. They'd pick up riches like a rabbit picks up ticks. That was their skill.

My father's six cousins and his uncle were amongst the first to leave. His uncle did not say to father, "You are family. So is the girl. You both must come with us. I promised your dying mother years ago that I'd look after you." He simply disappeared at night.

When traders left, the stoneys squabbled over who should occupy their homes. The victors lived in grandeur without food and with no purpose to their lives. They maintained walls, of course. They observed the rigid courtesies of life. They made no noise at night. And there were some who still sat at their anvils working flint as if they thought that bronze, brought in by boat, would tire of us and go to sea again.

The wiser ones sat on the stones outside their homes to warm themselves in winter light. Why waste good wood on heating flint? They needed all the wood for night when, opened by their hunger to the cold, they could not sleep. They were not tired. Their muscles were unused. They had not spent the day silently engaged with stone. For once, low conversations filled the night. What if? What if? What if we stay here, will we live? What if we leave, what then?

And in the day what was there else to do but talk? The

village seemed a shabby and a friendly place at last. People did not shut themselves inside. They strolled. They lingered. They paused for chat and gossip and for news. They took an interest in each other's grieving, empty inside worlds and in the outside world as well. How could they not? The outside world was closing in like lichen on a stone. Unless the stone is busy, turning all day long, the lichen creeps and clothes and wraps. And so the hill, the forest and the sea wrapped us up too. The paths became unused, the pits fell in, the wind reorganized our lives. We lived like rabbits, sociable and bored and easy prey.

When horsemen came we hid. They did not come, of course, for arrow-heads, or tools. They only came to ride between our homes and to shout obscenities and threats. They were our masters now. Some nights they used an empty merchant's house for stables and for sleep. They drank, and were as rash and ragged as small boys. We feared the time when they would help themselves to women or to food. Was it in our lifetime or just a dream when stoneys had told such riders to dismount and leave their horses in the care of boys, when we could turn our backs on them and tell ourselves, "Anyone can ride a horse and shake a stick. Where is the skill in that?"

At last the truth was plain. My father broke his silence to pass his wisdom on. "So now you know," he said. "You can't eat stone. You can't burn stone. You can't make clothes from flint. You'll have to leave this village or you'll die." His audience told him, "Hold your tongue." They preferred – we all preferred – the entertainment of his lies.

31

WE TOOK OUR LEAVE IN spring. There were old people there, too frail to walk. They chose to stay behind and take their chances in the village of their births. They would not be alone. There were the horsemen who passed through and might be grateful for some help with caring for their mounts or cooking food. A pair of sisters and their stoney men refused to leave as well. They'd spoken – or much more – with passing merchants. They thought that they'd survive by living off the trees. The merchants promised that they'd trade food for charcoal. The cost of charcoal was too high near where the bronze was made.

Leaf stopped behind as well. He hadn't give up on flint. Through all the hunger and decay he'd stayed at work, producing blades. But now his box of tools had bronze amongst the antler tines and wood. He had no time to ponder on the irony of that. He only knew this fact – that bronze was tough and sharp. His spike of bronze when placed upon the fracture point of flint and hammered with some wood was better than a tine for separating tool from stone. He found he could make his perfect and unwanted flints more easily with bronze.

We left him there behind his draughtless walls, so focused on his anvil and his stone that our departure could force few farewells – and no tears – from him. He thought we were the foolish ones. He saw no sense in flight.

My father was restored to noise and health. At last he was in charge. As soon as it was clear that village life was dead and that the stoneys had to leave, who else was there to show the way but father? They all recalled the times he told them what life was like beyond the village and the hill. Their little liar was to be their guide. He was a young man once again, despite his weeping arm, despite the flaking of his face, despite the stretched and stringy tresses on his mouth and tongue. He leapt. And called. And danced. He made promises that they would find a world more lively than the one they'd known. He was the sporting porpoise that always leads the school.

The school was more subdued. The villagers were weighed down by bags and slings and sleds. They'd packed each scrap of food or cloth, each pot, each tool, each skin as if they thought that their new world would match the old. They did not know what travel meant. Most had never been beyond the hill before. They carried children in their arms. They seemed to think their journey was a stroll. To where? Who knows? The stoneys dared not guess. They left it to my father to invent or find a route for them. So when he told them to leave their chattels and their sleds behind and carry only warm clothes, water, food, they did as they were asked. He told the parents, too, to carry nursing children in a sling and not across their arms. They'd need their hands and arms to fend off branches or to grasp on rocks or to spread like wings for balance when paths descended cliffs.

Leaf's house, his walls, were our last view of home. The chippings and the knappings that we heard from his workshop were our last village sound. Leaf stayed inside, at work. His labours were a rebuke to us all.

"Work is for the idle," father said. Our laughter gave us courage. We did what father had done all those years before. We simply filled our chests with air and set off down the coast.

You must have seen the way sheep move. We were like that. Our eyes were on the ground. There was no purpose in our step. Our faces were expressionless and worn. But, once we had passed by the flattened bracken where my mother's life and my father's arm were lost, there was something in the wind which made us lift our chins. The odour and the challenge of the sea, perhaps. The salt. The mewling of the gulls, distressed and fearful that we were hunting for their eggs. Or something else? Or something more like joy. Our faces which were like the chalk that once had settled in our lungs became like apples, shiny, fleshy, red. We looked about. The world was upside down, just as my father said. The gulls had backs. The shallows of the sea were edged with arcs of phlegm. The wind was low enough to touch and cup inside our palms. We'd thought the sea was flat – but now we gazed upon its trenches and its peaks. It seemed as solid as a hill.

The flock of sheep quite soon became a line of goats, adept at finding ways which skirted brambles, gorse and winkle-berries. The stoneys found that feet and legs could bounce, that songs and whistles and wisecracks could well involuntarily from their mouths, that there were rewards to be had in doing simple things.

We stopped to drink and eat what food we had brought at the stream amongst the boulders by the beach. Leaf, the village, flints, were only half a day behind. But none of us looked back along the coast. We had our greedy eyes upon the undulating path which led up from the stream, through mallow, bracken, moss, into the clouds and sky. The only mentions people made of the village that they'd left were jokes at Leaf's expense. "He didn't dare to walk with us into the wind," they said, "for fear his hair would blow away. Some gull would take his bald head for an egg and use it as a nest." And they repeated father's joke that work is for the idle. It pleased them more than anything he'd said.

That evening – more weary than we'd ever been – we came to lowlands which were unlike the landscapes we had known – except, we recognized this place from stories father told. Low heathland swept gently to the shore where thrift and black-tufted lichens lived side by side on rocks with barnacles and limpets. There were clumps of seablite, flourishing on spray. There was arrow grass and milkwort. All the herbs and medicines and vegetables that we had seen bunched up for barter in the market-place were in abundance here.

Do not imagine that I felt that this was home or that I ran in search of where my mother's hut had been. I was too young – and tired – for sentiment. I lay down by the fire they'd made and slept. And while I slept the stoneys gathered food while father pointed with his hand at what was good to eat and what was bad. He challenged boys and girls to bring some rabbits back. He went with neighbours, hunting eggs. He showed how samphire should be pulled and cooked.

The stoneys could not stick at any task. They were like dragonflies, first here, then there, then by the water's edge. It was not long before someone picked up a juice-red, elderberry rock and – half recalling tales that father told – flung it to the ground. It fell apart. No piece of it was larger than a plum. Soon other stoneys gathered round. They clapped their hands in glee. They'd never seen such soft and useless stone before. They squatted on the beach like children, crumbling stone on stone, reducing rock to shingle, grit and blood-red sand. Some kept the larger pieces for good luck.

That night we gathered at the fire and shared out all the food. It did not matter that some hunters had had no luck with rabbits or with eggs. A shared pot shares out luck as well. There was a little talk of how our lives might be but mostly there was sleep.

My father's arm was at its worst at night. He stood with his back to the fire and hugged his stump with his one hand. He would have stayed like that all night, except he heard me calling out his name. I was unnerved by what I thought were wolves. I'd heard a cough or barking coming from the heath. We listened, and at last we heard the sound again, the faintest summons from far off.

"It's only foxes," father said, and then, unable to resist the lie, "Listen, and you'll hear the seals. You'll hear them barking at the foxes in reply."

Once more we listened to the night. The next bark that we heard was full of salt and came in on the wind.

My father did not smile. At last his lies had caught him out. He knew what no one else had guessed, that this salt heath was the limit of his knowledge of the outside world, that all he knew of better days was those few times with Doe. He looked out at the night beyond the heath where, next day, we would go. The stars were just the same, the moon, the wind. No doubt they had a sun there too. The stories that he'd told were now our past. His new task was to invent a future for us all. He closed his eyes and what he saw was the shingled margin of the sea with horses wild and riderless close by. He tried to place a sail upon the sea, but could not. He tried to fill the air with human sounds. But all he saw were horses in the wind, the tide in loops upon the beach, the spray-wet rocks and stones reflecting all the changes in the sky, and no one there to notice or applaud.